First published in Canada in 2009 by
McArthur & Company
322 King St. West, Suite 402
Toronto, Ontario
M5V 1J2
www.mcarthur-co.com

Designed by Kato Wake www.katowake.com
Bottle photos by Doug Hall
Other photos by Billy Munnelly/Kato Wake

Printed in Canada by Webcom

The publisher would like to acknowledge the financial support of the Government of Canada through the Book Publishing Industry Development Program (BPIDP) and the Canada Council for our publishing activities. The publisher further wishes to acknowledge the financial support of the Ontario Arts Council and the OMDC for our publishing program.

10 9 8 7 6 5 4 3 2 1

Contact Billy Munnelly at
billysbestbottles@gmail.com

Mixed Sources
Product group from well-managed forests, and other controlled sources
www.fsc.org Cert no. SW-COC-002358
© 1996 Forest Stewardship Council
FSC

BILLY'S BEST BOTTLES

WINES FOR 2010

McArthur & Company
Toronto

ABOUT THE AUTHOR

Billy Munnelly has been drinking and critiquing wine full-time for more than twenty-five years. His concepts for understanding wine have helped thousands to overcome wine angst and get more fun out of the subject. Billy never uses wine jargon or confusing gobbledygook – wines are described in everyday terms. Born in Ireland, he originally trained in the hotel and restaurant industry. A self-confessed former gourmet, he now prefers the celebration of everyday pleasures. Munnelly lives in Toronto and Prince Edward County with his partner Kato Wake, who designed this book.

FOLLOW BILLY ON HIS BLOG:
www.billysbestbottles.com

ON FACEBOOK:
facebook.com/billysbestbottles

ON TWITTER:
twitter.com/billymunnelly

ABOUT THIS BOOK

BILLY'S BEST BOTTLES WINES FOR 2010 FEATURES **MORE THAN 200 REALLY GOOD WINES – MOST OF THEM IN THE $10 TO $16 RANGE.**

EACH RECOMMENDATION COMES WITH A **COLOUR PHOTO OF THE BOTTLE** AND **ITS CODE NUMBER** – WHICH IS **APPLICABLE CANADA-WIDE.**

THE WINES ARE **CATEGORIZED BY MOOD AND SITUATION**, SO YOU'LL KNOW THEIR **BEST USE**.

ALL STYLES OF WINE ARE COVERED – DRY, SWEET, LIGHT AND RICH.

MORE THAN 1500 WINES WERE TASTED – AND MANY WERE CONSUMED – WHILE COMPILING THIS BOOK.

BESIDES BEST WINE BUYS, YOU'LL FIND **INFORMATION ON GRAPES, WINE AND FOOD PAIRINGS, ENTERTAINING AND MY FAMOUS "20 STEPS TO WINEDOM"**.

THIS IS THE **20TH EDITION OF BILLY'S BEST BOTTLES HANDBOOK**.

THIS BOOK IS **DESIGNED TO MAKE WINE CHOICES AS EASY AS GROCERY SHOPPING**. FIRST YOU THINK ABOUT WHAT YOU NEED, THEN YOU BUY A WINE FROM THAT CATEGORY.

BILLY'S BEST BOTTLES WINES FOR 2010

CONTENTS

20 YEARS OF THIS BOOK

A SHORT HISTORY

The first edition was published in 1989, in Stratford, Ontario. Entitled *How to Buy a Bottle,* it featured two wine characters: J. P. Knoselotts (the snob) and L. Bo Bender (the hero) and their banter at the LCBO. Recommended wines included TORRES SANGRE DE TORO ($6.95) and CAMPOFIORIN ($11.60). I printed ten times too many copies – not a good start at self-publishing.

I continued with the two characters in '90, and the book had 75 pages and sold for $8.95. But of course I printer fewer copies. Chile and Argentina were predicted to be upcoming stars, and SEGURA VIUDAS made its first of many appearances.

In 1991 the title became *The Best Bottles Wine Handbook*, and changed the format to a square shape with a hard cover and spiral binding. And fired the two wine characters. First appearances for WOLF BLASS YELLOW LABEL ($13.60), LEON BEYER PINOT GRIS ($12.55) and HARDYS TRAMINER/ RIESLING ($8.75).

In '93 I asked the LCBO if they would sell my book but was told that some of the illustrations were "potentially offensive". "And so are a lot of your wines, so I guess we're even."

DUBEOUF BEAUJOLAIS ($10.65) and LA VIEILLE FERME ($8.20) made their first appearance.

Because the Board said no, I decided to enlarge the illustrations in the next issue. And I shortened the title to *Best Bottles,* with my name in BOLD. Friends told me to do this. In '95 I embarked upon a new tactic to generate sales. My picks were offered in the form of a diary – one or two wines for each week of the year. Diaries were hot so why not fill one with wine tips? ALIANCA BAIRRADA ($7.50) was now a five-year veteran of my book.

Around this time I realized that selling a book was a bigger task than writing one. My original goal of 20,000 copies was starting to look a bit ambitious. I continued in diary format in '96 and '97 and added shopping lists, tips and just about anything that I thought would entice buyers. It was a good period – *Billy's Best Bottles* became the name of the book, and I celebrated ten years of my *Billy's Best Bottles Wineletter* (another story) with a big bash in my Stratford backyard. CONO SUR PINOT NOIR ($7.85), FETZER ZINFANDEL ($10.85) and VINELAND DRY RIESLING ($9.40) made their debuts. All the books

up to this date were printed by *Commercial Printers* in Stratford, but in 1997 I made the mistake of going elsewhere for a better price. Dealing with a big firm in another province resulted in poor communication and product – the books arrived three weeks late. And you have no idea how upset neighbours get when an eighteen-wheeler delivery truck from Quebec backs up on their lawn!

In '98 I decided to get back to basics – an edition with my own photographs, printed locally. I should mention that in this era, the party-friendly graphic firm called *Creative Feats* was my savior as I struggled between individual expression and good design. (Thanks Heidi and Karen.) Hot new wines at this time were CHATEAU DES CHARMES ALIGOTE ($10.95), VILLA MARIA SAUVIGNON ($12.70), CH. DE GOURGAZAUD ($9.95) and lots of stuff from CALITERRA in Chile.

By now I was up to 165 pages, with a selling price of $18 (including shipping). The dairy concept was scrapped because I learned that

stores had difficulty selling my book after January. Not a big deal because I was starting to develop the concept of mood/situation categories for wine buying (originally called the ABC system).

Everyone wanted to do something special for Y2K so I went with a crazy cover and an action-packed book? Chilean wines were big that year – lots of CALITERRA, SANTA RITA, CARMEN and ERRAZURIZ.

My next innovative move was the put the '01 edition in a box to appeal to the gift market. The box included a separate booklet of wine tips – and a pencil, and had a colourful, cubist art cover. Looked great – should have won a packaging award! But the firm supplying the boxes went out of business, and it was almost year-end before I found another source. I lost a lot of Christmas sales. Can I sell you a pencil?

A better idea surfaced in '02 – I put the distribution of my book in the hands of Whitecap Books, who had just published books with Jamie Kennedy and Inn on the Twenty restaurant. The '02-'03 years marked a great improvement in sales and design. The label/bottle images were looking better thanks to technology, a great printer (*Topknotch*) and my partner and graphic artist, Kato Wake. The '03 book had a laminated cover that was so sharp you could shave with it! STONELEIGH SAUVIGNON ($12.30) and CESARI MERLOT ($6.50) were now on the scene. In '04 we switched to the current tall, thin, pocket-sized format. Easy to hold and easy to wrap with a wine bottle. GRÜNER VELTLINER ($9.95) appeared.

The most recent books have more pages to accommodate the glut of good wines. And instead of soaking bottles and scraping off labels we have the bottles photographed by a professional (Doug Hall). And after seventeen years of independence I signed on with the publishing house of McArthur and Company and got to party with other authors. My sales target is starting to look possible after all.

HELLO and welcome to the 20th edition of Billy's Best. I feel like an old rocker – hope they don't put me in some hall of fame!

It's been fun looking at the past editions and thinking about my annual improvement ideas and the schemes to boost sales. And the many all-nighters in the crunch week before printing. Would love to hear from those who purchased the first few editions. Typeset on a computer so primitive that the text appeared upside down on the screen. Corrections took hours.

Enough of the nostalgia. What's happening wine-wise in 2010? Australia has peaked, Chile and Argentina are the new hot spots, Italy is keeping the Old World in the game, and worldwide recession means tons of great values. Wineries are hurting but the drinker has never had it better. You can have a full wine life without ever spending more than $15. As you'll discover in this book.

My goal this year was to limit my picks to 100 but couldn't keep it that low. But I've been very selective and the number is just over 200 – a lot less than the past few years.

From the earliest days I've tried to offer more than just a list of good wine buys. I've been delighted by your positive feedback on my `Wine by Mood´ system of categorizing wine – and your desire to see it implemented in stores. There's tons of good wine out there, but it's knowing how to play them that creates the magic. Beware of anyone telling you that a wine is good without including a context, a mood.

Good local wines are endearing for sure, and there are almost 50 recommended in this book. But there could be a lot more if the LCBO allowed local wineries more retail access. Such as the VQA stores in British Columbia. The `Control´ word is not serving local.

Hope you enjoy my photos. Used to have them in the early books and thought it would add a light touch to the 20th. Twenty is, of course, the theme this year so look for: 20 Most Asked Wine Questions, 20 Wine Things I've Learned in 20 Years, 20 Steps to Winedom, and visit billysbestbottles.com for a chance to win a night at Niagara's Inn on the Twenty.

Billy's Best would never have succeeded had it not been for the core of supporters who saw me through the early years. And who came to all the parties. My big delight was discovering that many enjoyed and shared my playful approach to wine. And my big lesson from all of this is that you can create anything you want, if you want it enough.

Thanks to Kim and her fab crew at McArthur & Company for publishing and promoting this book. Love those Rosé business lunches. Thanks to copy-editor Laurel and to bottle photographer Doug, and to all the independent stores across the country that sell my book – I have a special fondness for what the independent spirit brings to life. And not to forget the winemakers and importers who support my work. Special thanks to Kato Wake – who not only designed this book, but provided insights into every aspect of its creation – especially the tasting. The best partner I could hope for. And lastly, thanks to my readers, for your inspiration and support.

Slainté,

Billy Munnelly   Toronto 2009

RICH BUT PLAYFUL TOO

Rich reds often wonder into heaviness and become overbearing, or boring. **RAVENSWOOD ZINFANDEL** goes in another direction – ending up **bright, lively and playful. And it's mighty charming.** Get a bottle, get a date and start playing.

wine style: RICH RED
RAVENSWOOD 07 ZINFANDEL 'VINTNERS BLEND', CALIFORNIA
259257 VE $17.95 page 174

PUTTING ON A GOOD SHOW

ARANCIO is the Sicilian branch plant of the very good **MEZZACORONA** winery, located in the north of Italy. The newly arrived white **'GRILLO'** (name of the grape) and **SYRAH** offer quality, a hit of Italy and good drinkability. Invite them over this weekend.

wine style: NICE & EASY WHITE
ARANCIO 08 GRILLO, SICILY
114710 $11.75 page 93

GET DOWN WITH D'ARENBERG

While Aussie reds are never short on flavour and richness, they can lack the guts, edge or earthiness that **challenges the imagination and refreshes the palate.** But not so with **'D'ARRY'S ORIGINAL'** which has the crusty character of traditional wines. Bravo.

wine style: RICH RED

DARENBERG 06 SHIRAZ/GRENACHE 'D'ARRY'S ORIGINAL', MCLAREN VALE, AUSTRALIA 942904 VE $19.75 page 200

GREAT LOCAL EXPRESSION FROM COYOTE'S RUN

For me, **local is interesting when it tastes different than all the other wines in the world.** The folks at **COYOTE'S RUN** have put a local spin on the two wines featured in this book – especially their Cabernet.

wine style: NICE & EASY WHITE

COYOTE'S RUN 08 PINOT GRIS/PINOT BLANC, VQA ONTARIO 112144 $15.75 page 97

wine style: RUSTIC RED

COYOTE'S RUN 07 CABERNET, VQA NIAGARA 26757 $16.30 page 152

HOT, NEW & HAPPENING

PERKY PINOT

Most know Pinot Noir as a charming, sensual experience but the original from Burgundy can be quite tart. That's how the locals like it – they understand how **tartness stimulates the appetite and lifts flavours out of food.** Try the **MUCH IMPROVED PATRIARCHE 07 PINOT.**

wine style: RUSTIC RED
PATRIARCHE 07 PINOT NOIR, BURGUNDY, FRANCE
23903 $16.25 page 145

GET ON THE GOURGAZAUD

There seems to be a **bistro revival** – affordable food and wines offered in a simple setting with the focus on having fun. **CH. DE GOURGAZAUD** is a **classic bistro red** – country wildness meets big nourishment. Rustic meets easy drinking.

wine style: RUSTIC RED
CH. DE GOURGAZAUD 07
MINERVOIS, FRANCE
22384 $12.80 page 146

START WITH STARBUCKS, FINISH WITH SEGURA

We're familiar with the morning coffee habit but **we need to cultivate the evening bubbly habit.** Having a glass of inexpensive sparkling wine offers a transition between work and home life. **An opened, refrigerated bottle will stay fresh for a week and provide you with a glass a day.** **SEGURA VIUDAS HAS BEEN IN ALL 20 EDITIONS OF THIS BOOK!**

(Note to self: buy a champagne stopper!)

wine style: FRESH WHITE
SEGURA VIUDAS BRUT, SPAIN 158493 $14.95 page 55

GRANGE ON GAMAY

wine style: LIVELY RED
THE GRANGE 07 GAMAY 'TRUMPOUR'S MILL', VQA PRINCE EDWARD COUNTY
615062 $14.80 page 119

THE GRANGE is one of **Prince Edward County's showpiece wineries** – set in a huge, restored barn by a millpond. For a picture of the place, pick up a bottle of their **GAMAY 'TRUMPOUR'S MILL'.** Fruity, tart and refreshing – just as Gamay should be. **Visit the winery for excellent 07 Cab Franc and Pinot Noir.**

HOT, NEW & HAPPENING

CONO SUR:

THE WONDER WINERY

One of the aims of **CONO SUR** is to make **really good, everyday-priced editions** of exclusive wines such as **Pinot Noir** and **Viognier**. And they have succeeded. Another cause for celebration is their **LUSH AND SEDUCTIVE TEN-DOLLAR SHIRAZ.** Too good for words.

wine style: RICH RED
CONO SUR 08 SHIRAZ, CHILE 64295 $9.95 page199

CARMEN HAS THE TOUCH!

CARMEN'S CHARDONNAY, MERLOT and **CABERNET** have the ripe, bright flavours of hot climate wine, but there's also a light-handed touch. A little French-ness. **You can drink lots.** Maybe a second bottle – especially the Cabernet.

wine style: RICH RED
CARMEN 08 MERLOT, CHILE 248625 $10.70 page 164

wine style: RICH WHITE
CARMEN 08 CHARDONNAY, CHILE 235663 $9.70 page 109

wine style: RICH RED
CARMEN 07 CABERNET SAUVIGNON, CHILE 78980 $10.75 page 199

BOW DOWN TO BERNARD

You may have to bend all the way down to the bottom shelf to find the **CÔTES DU RHÔNE** of **LOUIS BERNARD**. But you'll end up going home with two of **THE MOST DELICIOUS AND UNDER-PRICED REDS IN THE STORE.**

wine style: RICH RED
LOUIS BERNARD 07 CÔTES DU RHÔNE-VILLAGES, FRANCE 391458 $12.85 page 197

wine style: RICH RED
LOUIS BERNARD 07 CÔTES DU RHÔNE, FRANCE 581645 $11.80 page 199

SOME BRANDS DO GET BETTER

When a wine has been around for as long as **MASI CAMPOFIORIN**, you have to ask the obvious question: **Is it still good? YES.** The current 06 vintage is one of the **BEST EVER.** Really deep flavours and brimming with vitality and confidence. A rockin' Ripasso.

wine style: RICH RED
MASI 06 VALPOLICELLA RIPASSO 'CAMPOFIORIN', VENETO, ITALY
155051 $17.45 page 170

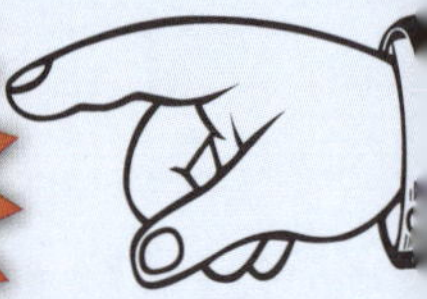

DEVILISHLY GOOD

One of the advantages of being a really big winery is the ability to offer a line of **quality wines at a good price. CONCHA Y TORO'S 'CASILLERO DEL DIABLO'** wines fall into this category, and their **Malbec, Carmenere** and **Shiraz** deliver character as well as value.

wine style: RICH RED

CONCHA Y TORO 08 CARMENERE 'CASILLERO DEL DIABLO', CHILE 620666 $12.95 page 167

CONCHA Y TORO 08 SHIRAZ 'CASILLERO DEL DIABLO', CHILE 568055 $12.95 page 189

CONCHA Y TORO 08 MALBEC 'CASILLERO DEL DIABLO', CHILE 94060 $12.95 page 187

NEW ROSÉ FROM THE SOUTH OF FRANCE

The need for a decent South of France Rosé has been filled by the arrival of **OGIER'S VENTOUX. Dry, semi-rich and a little earthy. Classic bistro-style.**

wine style: DRY ROSÉ

OGIER 08 ROSÉ VENTOUX, RHÔNE, FRANCE 134916 $11.95 page 117

THE ORIGINAL CHARDONNAY

In case your Wikipedia isn't working, let me tell you that Chardonnay originated in Burgundy, France. Here, they also discovered that putting wine in oak casks gave it an exotic touch – so they could charge big bucks. **LOUIS JADOT'S CHARDONNAY offers a hit of the original but at a reasonable price.**

wine style: RICH WHITE

LOUIS JADOT 07 CHARDONNAY, BURGUNDY, FRANCE
733077 VE $20.95 page 103

ALL THE RAGE IN PARIS

Here's a David and Goliath story. Nicolas Feuillatte is a relatively new Champagne producer who took on the long-established houses, and won. It has become the **NUMBER ONE SELLING CHAMPAGNE in Paris restaurants, and is the BEST PRICED CHAMPAGNE at the LCBO.**

wine style: FRESH SPARKLING

NICOLAS FEUILLATTE BRUT CHAMPAGNE, FRANCE 537605 $49.95 page 70

BRING IN THE JESTER

METOLO is a **newish Aussie winery that's über hot** – with monster reds at monster prices. Fortunately, they're kind enough to offer a $20 wine, more or less in the same vein, called **'JESTER'.**

wine style: RICH RED

MITOLO 07 SHIRAZ 'JESTER', MCLAREN VALE, AUSTRALIA 659607 $21.95 page 203

A CHILEAN WINERY DOING A VALUE VILLAGE

CALITERRA seems to be **on a crusade to deliver the best value wines in the world.** Love that kind of crusader! Their **CHARDONNAY, SAUVIGNON** and **CABERNET** are sure to get you excited. Check them out.

wine style: NICE & EASY WHITE

CALITERRA 09 SAUVIGNON BLANC RESERVA, CHILE 275909 $8.95 page 89

wine style: NICE & EASY WHITE

CALITERRA 08 CHARDONNAY RESERVA, CHILE 257147 $8.95 page 92

wine style: RICH RED

CALITERRA 08 CABERNET SAUVIGNON RESERVA, CHILE 257329 $8.95 page 190

MAKE FRIENDS WITH MEDOC

Bordeaux is the most prestigious red wine region in the world and home to the **CAB/MERLOT BLEND**. But everyday Bordeaux can be challenging because of its dry nature. Put it **with food, however, and the wine comes alive.** Or more to the point, it makes the food (especially beef) taste great. **Take the challenge with CALVET MEDOC.**

wine style: RUSTIC RED

CALVET 06 MEDOC, BORDEAUX, FRANCE 38208 $13.95 page 132

STRAWBERRY FIELDS

One of the **MOST FUN WINES ON THE PLANET** is the **strawberry-flavoured bubbly from Chile** called **FRESITA**. Made with real fruit. No cloying sweetness. Pour often. Everyone will love you.

wine style: SEMI-SWEET SPARKLING

VINA CASAL DE GORCHS 'FRESITA', CHILE 56697 $13.95 page 209

BRINGING BACK THE OLD ROMANTIC

Rioja was the original romantic red but it's gotten lost in today's crowded wine world. In the **Spanish section** pick up a bottle of **CAMPO VIEJO** and see how it can add a good feeling to any situation. Romantic or otherwise.

wine style: RUSTIC RED

CAMPO VIEJO 06 RIOJA CRIANZA, SPAIN
620997$14.45 page 145

SOFT ROCK SAUVIGNON

SAUVIGNON BLANC'S appeal is its wildness but there are situations when something a little more tame is better. **STONELEIGH** is **lively and refreshing without being over-the-top. A great party starter and food friendly too.** Check it out with asparagus risotto.

wine style: FRESH WHITE

STONELEIGH 08 SAUVIGNON BLANC, MARLBOROUGH, NEW ZEALAND

293043 $16.95 page 67

YOU SAY BISTRO, I SAY BBQ

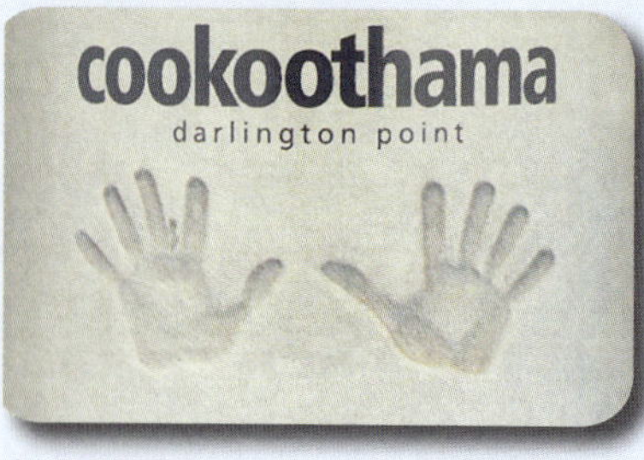

Australia is no longer strong on value but **Nugan Estate still over-delivers with its COOKOOTHAMA wines.** The **CHARDONNAY, SHIRAZ** and **CABERNET** have a solid bistro feeling. BBQ wines too, of course! Bring on the hot and spicy.

wine style: RICH WHITE
NUGAN ESTATE 07 CHARDONNAY, 'COOKOOTHAMA' AUSTRALIA
619403 $13.95 page 113

wine style: RICH RED
NUGAN ESTATE 07 CABERNET/MERLOT 'COOKOOTHAMA', AUSTRALIA
91660 $13.95 page 190

wine style: RICH RED
NUGAN ESTATE 07 SHIRAZ 'COOKOOTHAMA', AUSTRALIA
619460 $14.00 page 189

MY FAVOURITE BULL

One of the most **overlooked golden oldies at the LCBO is Spain's SANGRE DE TORO.** Even more friendly now that it's **screw cap** and the **07 MAY BE THE BEST EVER VINTAGE**. Twist open, pour and you'll discover a bright modern wine. Charming and seductive – much like Pinot. **TORRES SANGRE DE TORO** has been in **EVERY EDITION OF THIS BOOK**. A good-with-everything, red house wine.

wine style: RICH RED
TORRES 07 SANGRE DE TORO, CATALONIA, SPAIN
6585 $11.75 page 163

THE FETZER FEELING

FETZER has the knack for producing wines that combine **great drinkability with character**. Nice but real. Wines with a happy feeling. Freshen up your life with **FETZER'S SAUVIGNON BLANC.**

wine style: FRESH WHITE
FETZER 08 SAUVIGNON BLANC 'VALLEY OAKS', CALIFORNIA
34033 $12.45 page 65

GOOD OLD GUIGAL

When I started writing about wine **GUIGAL** was a little known producer. Today, **his single vineyard wines are ranked with the best in the world.** You can catch a little of the magic in his **CÔTES DU RHÔNE.**

wine style: RICH RED
GUIGAL 05 CÔTES DU RHÔNE, FRANCE
259721 $17.80 page 201

HOT, NEW & HAPPENING

THE ORVIETO REVIVAL

There's an **Orvieto revival** happening. **The original Italian white hero is staging a comeback.** Lively, fruity and dishing out the charm. Pour **RUFFINO'S ORVIETO** with your favourite chicken recipe.

wine style: NICE & EASY WHITE

RUFFINO 08 ORVIETO, UMBRIA, ITALY 31062 $11.50 page 78

VERY PORTUGUESE, VERY RUSTIC, VERY GOOD

There's a movement to produce **more modern style reds** in **Portugal** but the **traditionalists aren't giving up**. You'll find both styles in this book. Only time will tell which direction is best, meanwhile I suggest you **check out my favourite, ALIANCA BAIRRADA RESERVA.** Traditional for sure, but feels right for today.

wine style: RUSTIC RED

CAVE ALIANCA 06 BAIRRADA RESERVA, PORTUGAL 158741 $8.50 page 141

wine style: FRESH SPARKLING

WOLF BLASS BRUT 'YELLOW LABEL', AUSTRALIA 649996 $17.95 page 69

STEAK'S NEW PARTNER

MALBEC is solid and serious and set to join Cabernet as a favourite wine choice for steak. If you're giving, or are invited to, a **dinner party** I highly recommend including **CATENA MALBEC.**

wine style: RICH RED
CATENA 07 MALBEC, MENDOZA, ARGENTINA
478727 VE $19.95 page 159

MOMMESSIN ON A MISSION

There was a time when Mommessin reflected the bad side of French wine – dull and overexposed. But much has changed and **their current offerings of BEAUJOLAIS and CÔTES DU RHÔNE are delicious – and bargain-priced.**

wine style: LIVELY RED
MOMMESSIN 08 BEAUJOLAIS, FRANCE
313734 $11.25 page 123

wine style: LIVELY RED
MOMMESSIN 08 CÔTES DU RHÔNE 'LES EPICES', FRANCE
14829 $11.85 page 127

THE WOLFMAN DOES IT ALL

WOLF BLASS is best known for his lush **SHIRAZES, CABERNETS** and **CHARDONNAYS**. But have you tried his **SPARKLING**? **It's very good, very Champagne-ish. But party priced.**

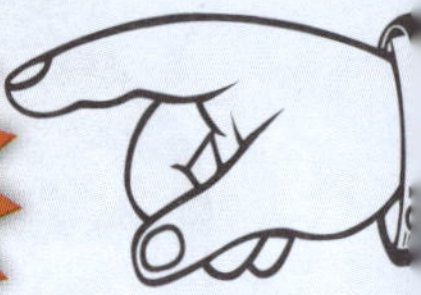

A IS FOR ALIGOTÉ

Low-flavoured white wines are enjoying a revival due to the popularity of Pinot Grigio. Some situations are best served by **modest, well-mannered wines.** A local contribution to this category is **CHATEAU DES CHARMES ALIGOTÉ. An excellent aperitif or hot day refresher.** It's one of the very few Aligotés made outside of France.

wine style: FRESH WHITE
CH. DES CHARMES 08 ALIGOTÉ, VQA NIAGARA-ON-THE-LAKE *284950 $13.25 page 68*

FIRST WITH A QR CODE

Congrats to **CHATEAU DES CHARMES for being the first local winery to put a QR CODE on their (new) packaging.** Just point your smart phone (iPhone or BlackBerry) and read all about the bottle in front of you. Maybe even my review of the wine! QR Codes and smart new labels – way to go!

wine style: FRESH WHITE
DUNAVAR 08 PINOT BLANC, HUNGARY 565820 $8.35 page 52

AN ONTARIO CLASSIC

Everyone said that **RIESLING** would never catch on with local drinkers. **CAVE SPRING CELLARS** has proven them wrong. Their wine is one of the bestsellers at the LCBO. Cave's trick is to **craft their Riesling in an off-dry style** – a hit of fruitiness to partner with Riesling's extreme tartness. **An anytime gulper.**

wine style: NICE & EASY WHITE

CAVE SPRING CELLARS 07 RIESLING, VQA NIAGARA 234583 $14.25 page 81

A NEW TAKE ON PINOT GRIGIO

Italy cornered a large portion of the white wine market with light, refreshing Pinot Grigio but it's now **adding another tier with richer editions. BARONE MONTALTO FROM SICILY** manages to feel both casual and special. Good before and with dinner.

wine style: RICH WHITE

BARONE MONTALTO 08 PINOT GRIGIO, SICILY
731148 $9.95 page 112

EXTEND YOUR TERRITORY

Hungarian wine (and food) used to be popular because it was cheap. Today there's another reason to buy Hungarian wine – it can be very good. **DUNAVAR PINOT BLANC delivers house wine refreshment and drinkability in the style of popular Pinot Grigio.** Ready when you are ready for a change.

HOT, NEW & HAPPENING

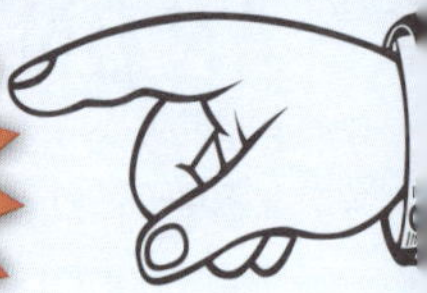

TECHNICOLOUR WINE!

I'll always remember my early experiences drinking **Californian Chardonnay.** A high for sure – **larger than life flavours**. Tasting **BERINGER'S STONE CELLARS CHARDONNAY** brought back these memories.

wine style: NICE & EASY WHITE

BERINGER 08 CHARDONNAY 'STONE CELLARS', CALIFORNIA 606806 $13.65 page 85

THE PEOPLE'S BUBBLY

The **Gallo winery** knows. That's why they are the largest in the world. At a weekend party most people enjoy wines that have a familiar name and are not bone-dry. Bring on **GALLO BUBBLY PINOT GRIGIO**. The Barefoot brand name reinforces the casual nature of this wine. Party on.

wine style: NICE & EASY SPARKLING

BAREFOOT BUBBLY PINOT GRIGIO, CALIFORNIA 106088 $12.95 page 79

HEY, GUESS WHAT LANDED...

(Hint: Not another Canada Goose.) **Pinot Noir is a temperamental superstar** – fussy about where it wants to touchdown. Who would have thought that a tiny island in Lake Erie would be a good landing spot?

MORE GAMAY PLEASE

I drink and pour a lot of Gamay and no one has ever complained. But wineries have a hard time selling it to the rest of you. Maybe a **lightly chilled bottle** of **ANGELS GATE GAMAY** could convert you. Have it early in the evening when you're ready for a lively red. Especially wonderful in the summer or with Thanksgiving turkey.

wine style: LIVELY RED
ANGELS GATE 07 GAMAY, VQA NIAGARA
107714 $12.95 page 119

GRAB THE GRÜNER

If you want to be cool you need to know the **Austrian white** made from the **GRÜNER VELTLINER grape.** It's this year's hot wine. **Expect the pure and refreshing quality of Riesling along with herbaceous or honey flavours.** A great way to start the evening. The solo LCBO offering, **WINZER KREMS,** has a delightful spring day feeling.

wine style: FRESH WHITE
WINZER KREMS 08 GRÜNER VELTLINER, AUSTRIA 589002 $10.75 page 53

...IN LAKE ERIE?

PELEE'S 08 PINOT delivers a gutsy edition that's bargain-priced.

wine style: RUSTIC RED
PELEE ISLAND 08 PINOT NOIR RESERVE, VQA PELEE ISLAND
135939 $14.75 page 136

COMING TO YECLA

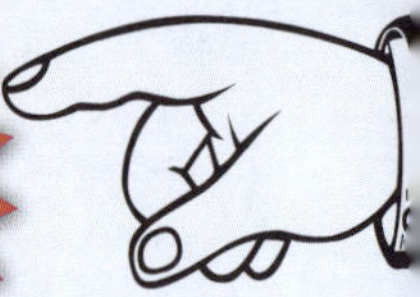

Look out Chile and Argentina. There's a new red from Spain that could give you serious competition. **LA CASONA** from the Yecla region is loaded with flavour but there's a peppery, earthy quality that reminds me of hearty reds from the south of France. **Certainly has the talent to challenge the current bestsellers.** Grab a bottle, or a case, for your casona.

wine style: RICH RED

BODEGAS CASTANO 07 'LA CASONA', MONASTRELL, YECLA, SPAIN 143743 $8.95 page 199

NICEST OF THE NICE WHITES!

Non-oaked Chardonnay is the nice girl/guy of wines. Welcome at almost every social event. Our local wineries do well with this style – it's the Canuck thing! **HILLEBRAND'S 'ARTIST SERIES' UNOAKED CHARDONNAY could take the prize for the nicest of the nice.** A yummy glass of wine with a nice label too.

wine style: NICE & EASY WHITE

HILLEBRAND ESTATES 08 UNOAKED CHARDONNAY 'ARTIST SERIES', VQA NIAGARA 83385 $10.95 page 84

ONE OF NIAGARA'S BEST JUST BECAME MORE AVAILABLE

You can now buy the Burgundy inspired (and seriously good) **LE CLOS JORDANNE** wines at **Wine Rack stores. Stunning CHARDONNAY** and **PINOT NOIR** at $25 and up.

wine style: RICH RED

LE CLOS JORDANNE 06 PINOT NOIR, 'VILLAGE RESERVE', VQA NIAGARA

Wine Rack Stores $25 page 175

wine style: RICH WHITE

LE CLOS JORDANNE 06 CHARDONNAY, VILLAGE RESERVE, VQA NIAGARA

Wine Rack stores $25.00 page 110

ARRIVE IN STYLE

Sometimes looks are important. **When taking a bottle to a fancy dinner you need a classy wine in a classy package.** Something fitting for the occasion. Such as the tall, dark and handsome **TRIUS RED. A premium local red with a great track record. Canadian wine, Italian bottle design, Aussie winemaker – a recipe for success.**

wine style: RICH RED

HILLEBRAND 07 TRIUS RED, VQA NIAGARA

303800 VE $21.95 page159

WHAT IS THIS SEREGO ALIGHIERI ROSSO?

Italians love to confuse us with their creativity. But it's often worth the effort to try and figure out the plot. **SEREGO ALIGHIERI** is a **deluxe Valpollicella** with a little **Sangiovese** (grape) added for vigour. It's not a Ripasso, so the fruit flavours are bright and lively, but it has spent time in cherry wood casks for a little spicy smoothness. **I love the play between exuberance and gentleness.**

wine style: RICH RED
SEREGO ALIGHIERI 07 ROSSO DEL VERONESE, VENETO, ITALY 447326 $15.75 page 179

THE BEAUTY OF THE BLEND

It's taken a while but local wineries have at last realized that a splash of Gewurztraminer does wonders for sales. It adds **a touch of sweetness and exotic flavouring** to the more neutral grape varieties. Check out **MALIVOIRE WHITE** – a blend of Chardonnay, Rielsing and Gewurz. Really, really nice wine.

wine style: NICE & EASY WHITE
MALIVOIRE 08 WHITE, VQA NIAGARA
141531 $14.9 5 page 97

NEDERBURG: A GOOD AMBASSADOR FOR SOUTH AFRICA

Every country or region needs a big winery to serve as an ambassador. Someone to deliver **quality at affordable prices**, with wines that **express local character. NEDERBURG** is doing this with their **'WINEMASTER'S SELECT' line.** I'll be amazed if you're not converted.

wine style: NICE & EASY WHITE
NEDERBURG 08 SAUVIGNON BLANC 'WINEMASTER'S RESERVE', SOUTH AFRICA
283713 $10.95 page 89

wine style: RICH RED
NEDERBURG 07 SHIRAZ 'THE WINEMASTER'S RESERVE', SOUTH AFRICA
527457 $10.95 page 177

wine style: RICH RED
NEDERBURG 07 CABERNET SAUVIGNON 'THE WINEMASTER'S RESERVE', SOUTH AFRICA 111526 $10.95 page 177

MR. BOUCHARD MAKES GOOD BISTRO BEAUJOLAIS

BOUCHARD AÎNÉ & FILS 08 BEAUJOLAIS is a **little fuller and more rustic** than usual. It's the kind of wine that millions of French have with their bistro suppers. **Enjoy with gusto** – Beaujolais doesn't do moderation.

wine style: RUSTIC RED
BOUCHARD AÎNÉ & FILS 08 BEAUJOLAIS SUPÉRIEUR, FRANCE
9431 $12.45 page 139

LIGHT 'N LIVELY LAMBERTI

Italian producer LAMBERTI shows a delicate touch with their **SANTEPIETRI wines**. Very café-ish, very everyday and very gulpable. Check out the light 'n lively **Pinot Noir.**

wine style: LIVELY RED
LAMBERTI 08 VALPOLICELLA 'SANTEPIETRE', VENETO, ITALY 560508 $11.25 page 129

wine style: LIVELY RED
LAMBERTI 07 PINOT NOIR 'SANTEPIETRE', VENEZIE, ITALY
74070 $11.95 page 125

TAKE MERLOT OUT OF THE DOG HOUSE

Merlot may be unfashionable but I'm still drinking it. Met this **DOG HOUSE 'MAXIE'S MERLOT'** at a party and now we're best friends. Cuddly richness but I mainly like its playfulness. A good party guest for sure.

wine style: RICH RED
DOG HOUSE 06 'MAXIE'S MERLOT', CALIFORNIA 614156 $13.75 page 164

ABRUZZI DOES WHITE TOO

By now most of you are familiar with the excellent and under-priced reds from the **Abruzzi region in the centre of Italy.** But check out their whites too. The newly arrived **SPINELLI PINOT GRIGIO** delivers more bright flavours and refreshment than you might expect for the price. **Lighthearted for the party scene but there's enough character for the supper table too.**

wine style: NICE & EASY WHITE

SPINELLI 08 PINOT GRIGIO, ABRUZZI, ITALY 113886 $8.95 page 91

THE HEARTBEAT OF ITALY

Traditional Chianti can appear to be out of sync with today's lifestyle. It's very dry, doesn't have great opening lines and appears rustic and wild. **Invite it to the dinner table, however, and you'll experience its food flattering ability and its talent for engaging your imagination – the original purpose of wine. EXPLORE ROCCA DELLE MACIE'S 'VERNAIOLO'** with Tuesday night pasta and the **'CLASSICO'** with a special weekend dinner.

wine style: RUSTIC RED

ROCCA DELLE MACIE 08 CHIANTI 'VERNAIOLO', TUSCANY, ITALY
269589 $13.45 p.138

wine style: RICH RED

ROCCA DELLE MACIE 08 CHIANTI 'CLASSICO', TUSCANY, ITALY 3962 $23.95 page 161

BILLY'S BEST BOTTLES

WINE BY MOOD CATEGORIES

Categories make subjects manageable by creating groupings. When we learn a few groupings then we know what to expect from the hundreds or thousands of choices. And categories tell us where things fit in relation to each other. Life would be way too chaotic without them. Currently stores offer wines by country but I think that mood/situation categories would do a better job in helping us select the wine that's going to work best. Food, clothing and household stores group items of a similar nature regardless of their place of origin. The following is my groupings for wine – all the wines in the world simplified to six categories: three for white and three for red.

Fr FRESH WHITE | **Ne** NICE & EASY WHITE | **Ri** RICH WHITE

WINE BY MOOD

WHITE WINE CATEGORIES

FRESH –NICE 'N EASY – RICH

1. The mood to be refreshed – with a white wine that feels FRESH. To get a party started or to quench our thirst on a hot day, we need a zesty white – one that feels FRESH. Even jolting. Wine that feels like a crunchy green apple or a squeeze of lime.

2. The mood for relaxation – with a white wine that feels NICE & EASY. A friendly and social drink. An EASY wine to have while we sip 'n chat or cook a weeknight meal. This wine category could be likened to Top 40 music or blue jeans – something that makes us feel comfortable.

3. The mood for a big experience – with a white wine that feels RICH. RICH whites satisfy our desire for something special, or romantic.

WINE BY MOOD
RED WINE CATEGORIES
LIVELY – RUSTIC – RICH

1. The mood to be refreshed – with a red wine that feels light and LIVELY. LIVELY reds are similar to FRESH whites – that's why they're served lightly chilled. Beaujolais is the best-known example and it's perfect for summer picnics, lunches and parties.

2. The mood for gusto – with a red wine that feels RUSTIC. Pizza, pasta, sausages and other everyday Italian foods are gutsy and down-to-earth, so they work well with wines of a similar nature – RUSTIC reds. RUSTIC wines have a bite to them and are also the perfect partner for burgers or white meats.

3. The mood to be nourished and comforted – with a red wine that feels RICH. The wine for steak and most rich foods. RICH reds nourish us with their warmhearted feeling. They hit a mellow, comfy chord in the same way as late night jazz.

☞ **PICK YOUR MOOD**

Where do you want to be on the spectrum?

☞ **THEN CHOOSE YOUR WINE FROM THE SELECTIONS OFFERED UNDER THAT MOOD CATEGORY**

(ie: if you're in the mood to be refreshed, then select a wine from the FRESH category)

W Ne NICE & EASY

FRIENDLY
SOCIAL

AKA
THE NICE GUY/GIRL

Have a nice time!

the mood to **cruise** *with white wine*

R Li LIVELY

LIGHTHEARTED
REFRESHING

AKA
THE PLAYFUL ONE

Lighten up!

the mood to **refresh** *with red wine*

W Fr FRESH

LIVELY
REFRESHING

AKA
THE LIVE WIRE

Let's get started!

the mood to **refresh** *with white wine*

Fr FRESH

ALIGOTÉ
BRUT SPARKLING
CHABLIS
NON-OAKED CHARDONNAY
DRY RIESLING
GRÜNER VELTLINER
MUSCADET
ORVIETO
PINOT GRIGIO (some)
SANCERRE
SAUVIGNON BLANC (some)
SOAVE
TREBBIANO
VERDICCHIO
VINHO VERDE

FOOD IDEAS

Antipasto, Oysters, Sole, Snapper, Sushi, Goat Cheese, Smoked Salmon, Thai Curries

Ne NICE & EASY

CHARDONNAY (some)
CHENIN BLANC
GEWURZTRAMINER (some)
MACON-VILLAGES
OFF-DRY RIESLING
PINOT BLANC
PINOT GRIGIO (some)
PINOT GRIS
RESERVE RIESLING
RUEDA
SAUVIGNON BLANC (some)
SEMILLON
VIOGNIER

FOOD IDEAS

Chicken, Turkey, Pork, Ham, Veal, Fish, Seafood, Egg Dishes, Pasta in Cream Sauce

Li LIVELY

BEAUJOLAIS
GAMAY
CÔTES DU RHÔNE (some)
CHIANTI (some)
MONTEPULCIANO D'ABRUZZO
MERLOT (cool climate)
CABERNET FRANC (cool climate)
PINOT NOIR (cool climate)
ROSÉ
VALPOLICELLA
ZWEIGELT

FOOD IDEAS

Roast Chicken, Mushroom Risotto, Tapas, Sandwiches, Picnic Food, Grilled Salmon, Indian Curry, Cajun Food, Tex Mex, Tuna & Swordfish

WWW.BILLYSBESTBOTTLES.COM

WINE BY MOOD *spectrum*

R **Ru** RUSTIC
GUTSY
INVIGORATING
AKA
THE DOWN-TO-EARTH TYPE
Pass da pasta!

the mood to go for **gusto** *with red wine*

W **Ri** RICH
GENEROUS
SEDUCTIVE
AKA
THE GLAMOUR GIRL
Where's my lobster?

the mood to **schmooze** *with white wine*

CHANGE YOUR MOOD
...CHANGE YOUR WINE!

R **Ri** RICH
WARMHEARTED
BIG & GENEROUS
AKA
THE BIG EASY
Where's my steak?

the mood to **schmooze** *with red wine*

Ru RUSTIC

BACO NOIR
BARBERA
CABERNET FRANC
CABERNET SAUVIGNON (cool climate)
CHIANTI
CÔTES DU RHÔNE (some)
MERLOT (cool climate)
LANGUEDOC
MARECHAL FOCH
MONTEPULCIANO D'ABRUZZO
PINOT NOIR
PORTUGUESE REDS
NAVARRA
SYRAH (some)
VALPOLICELLA

FOOD IDEAS
Pizza, Ribs, Sausages, Tomato Pasta, Burgers, Casseroles, BBQ'd Red Meat, Lasagna, Game, Roasted Vegetables

Ri RICH

OAKED CHARDONNAY
GEWURZTRAMINER
PINOT GRIS
SAUVIGNON BLANC (some)
SEMILLON
VIOGNIER

FOOD IDEAS
Salmon, Shellfish, Shrimp, Lobster, Roast Pork, Baked Ham, Rich Foods in Cream Sauce, BBQ'd White Meat & Fish, Hot & Spicy Dishes

Ri RICH

AMARONE
BAROLO
BORDEAUX
BRUNELLO
BURGUNDY (some)
CABERNET SAUVIGNON
CARMENERE
CHATEAUNEUF DU PAPE
CHIANTI RISERVA
CÔTES DU RHÔNE-VILLAGES
GRENACHE
MALBEC
MERITAGE
MERLOT
PORTUGUESE REDS (some)
RIOJA RESERVA
RIPASSO
SALICE SALENTINO
SHIRAZ
TEMPRANILLO
ZINFANDEL & PRIMITIVO

FOOD IDEAS
Steak, Lamb, Game, Roasts, Rich Braised Meats, Grilled or Roasted Meats

20 WINE THINGS I'VE LEARNED IN 20 YEARS

BILLY MUNNELLY

1 **There will always be more good wine than any of us can drink.**

2 **Wine culture is mainly about the superstars which creates the feeling that wines under $20 are just for poor people.** I've found that drinking upper-end wines is a lot like watching the game from a glass-enclosed box. Nice, but removed from the real action and grit of the game.

3 **The more you know about wine the harder it is to be open to new experiences.** We develop expectations and shun surprises. Don't be a knower.

4 **You'll have more fun if you let your heart and not your head rule your wine choices.**

5 **Instead of just looking for good wines, look for good wine relationships.** Combinations of wine, situation, mood, food, etc. **It's these relationships that create pleasure, not the wine itself. This is the most important thing I can tell you** – and naturally it's the focus of this book.

6 You will have more interesting drinking experiences if you **change the wine as often as you change the music.**

7 There is too much shine and glitz in winemaking. **Too many overworked, perfect wines.** A little imperfection and individual expression can add interest and make a wine feel real.

8 **Big wine glasses are best.** But don't attempt anything bigger than your head!

9 **The shift to screw cap is taking too long.** Shows the conservative nature of the wine industry.

10 **The North American palate has been calibrated on sweet drinks, food and sauces.** Soft wines with a touch of sweetness sell best in this market (Yellow Tail, Fuzion, etc.). **The European palate is more used to savoury and bitter foods** such as olives, tangy tomatoes and fresh herbs. Qualities that welcome rustic wines such as Sangiovese, Bordeaux and Bairrada.

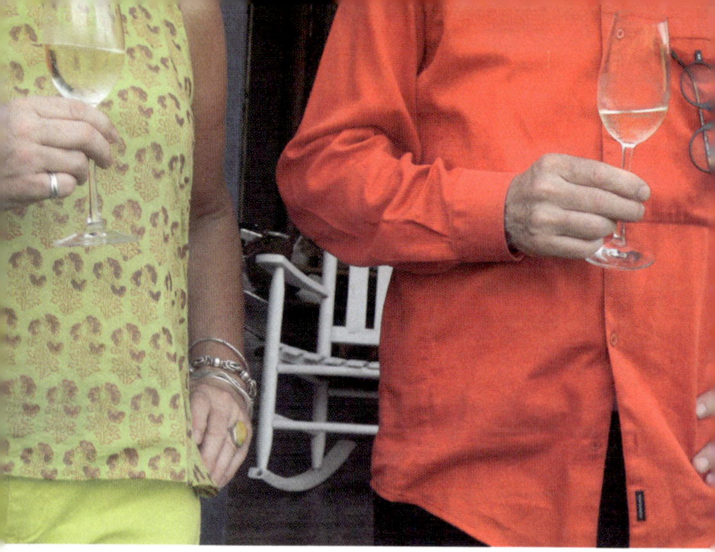

11 **We don't just taste wine, we have an experience with wine.** We feel something. Wine is an emotional experience. **Connect the feeling with the mood, and magic happens.** You do not need to know wine to enjoy it. If you can feel, you can be good `at wine'. And how does that make you feel? Fantastic I hope!

12 **Forget the details of the wine** you're tasting and concentrate on this question – in what situation might it give you pleasure? **What situation/mood would be enhanced by the wine? Ask this of every wine you taste.**

13 **Big wine companies often produce good wine and the small guys often screw up.**

14 **The consumer is not terribly interested in how, or where, wine (or anything) is made. They are mainly interested in "what it does for me".**

15 **Wine culture is closely aligned with café culture. Wine needs to be readily available, low-priced and down-styled. It needs to be inclusive.** Magazines which celebrate exculsive, high-priced wines in high-end settings deliver the wrong message.

16 **Scores are a lazy, meaningless way of interpreting wines.** Rich wines score high, as do smooth. Rustic and novel wines score low. But many of us prefer Bob Dylan to Michael Bublé.

17 **Guys seem to choose prestige wine. Girls seem to drink what they enjoy.**

18 **I drink everyday wines because they fit well with everyday life.** They fit in. There is room for food, conservation, etc. Grand and important wines dominate the situation.

19 While some might wish that there were less variety in wine, **it's the variety that makes it exciting**. And allows us to connect to life's endless variety of times, situations and moods.

20 **Put food, wine and people together and you will have a good time.**

BILLY'S BEST BOTTLES

WINES FOR 2010

Fr

FRESH

PARTY STARTER
THE OPENING ACT
REFRESHING
CITRUSSY
HOT DAY PATIO WINE
JOLTING
FOR APPETIZERS
FRESH & TART
HIGH ENERGY
LOW-FLAVOURED
THIRST-QUENCHING

FRESH
WHITES

HOT DAY IN JULY

One of my dream retirement projects would be to set up bars on the beaches of Europe and sell Vinho Verde. I'd use materials that suggested freshness – stone, stainless steel and maybe jazzy plastic to create a modern feeling. Green would be the main colour, of course.

Vinho Verde is the ultimate summer refresher because it's lighthearted, slightly spritzy and low in alcohol. Perrier with a kick. Keep an open bottle in your fridge and in your beach cooler.

Aveleda `Fonte´ is drier than in previous years and Sogrape's `Gazela' continues to be as refreshing as its package. But why not screw cap?

BEST TIMES: *A must-have for summer daytime and alfresco lunches.*

wine style: FRESH WHITE UNDER $12

AVELEDA 08 VINHO VERDE 'FONTE' PORTUGAL
5322 $8.95 / 238683 1500ml $16.45

wine style: FRESH WHITE UNDER $12

SOGRAPE VINHOS N/V VINHO VERDE 'GAZELA', PORTUGAL 141432 $8.95

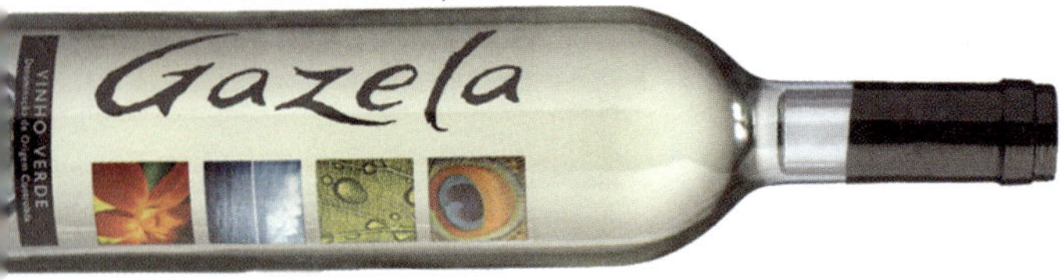

AUSSIE ROCKER AC/DC

Fr
FRESH WHITE

Are you up for adventure and a little headbanging? Australia's great contribution to white wine is the Semillon/Sauvignon blend (Sem-Sauv) as it offers a savoury alternative to the glut of overly fruity whites.

The main show in Sem-Sauv is bracing refreshment. The high volume character of AC/DC. Wine to get things going. Great stimulation at an everyday price. Other good features are low-alcohol and screw cap.

BEST TIMES: *As an aperitif, with seafood appetizers and generally revvvving up the senses.*

UNDER $12

wine style: FRESH WHITE
LONG FLAT WHITE 08 SEMILLON/SAUVIGNON, AUSTRALIA 183715 $10.75

EXTEND YOUR TERRITORY

Adventures in wine can be risky. You might be disappointed, waste your money, or worst of all, feel foolish in front of your buddies. None of this will happen to you because you've got my book – so it's safe to go on an adventure and buy a wine from Hungary. It will cost you all of eight dollars.

Young'uns out there might not know that Hungary used to be most people's first choice for everyday wines because they were low-priced and hearty. But hearty went out of fashion. Hungary is now attempting a comeback with lighter, fresher tasting wines. The Dunavar brand has been getting better each year and the 08 Pinot Blanc is an exuberant, low-flavoured refresher in the style of Pinot Grigio. But at a much lower price. Now in a new package with screw cap.

BEST TIMES: *Refresher or party starter.*

wine style: FRESH WHITE

DUNAVAR 08 PINOT BLANC, HUNGARY 565820 $8.35

UNDER $12

FYI: A sister wine,
DUNAVAR 08 MUSCAT-OTTONEL
(565812 $8.35) *is a super-tart, low-alcohol, hot day guzzler. Lip-smacking refreshment with just a hint of Muscat perfume.*

GRAB THE GRÜNER

Fr
FRESH WHITE

Here's another adventure. One that's guaranteed to please – especially in the summer. Grüner Veltliner is the national grape of Austria and up until recently they pretty much kept it to themselves. But now they're exporting small quantities for those who are smart enough to grab some.

Grüner expresses the feeling of Austria – mountain air, spring flowers – fresh and alive. There's also a little spritz, a little spice and a joyful feeling. Surely one of the most delightful white wines in the world. I've been recommending Winzer Krems Grüner for the past few years and the 08 vintage is the best yet.

BEST TIMES: *Anytime you're thirsty. Summer parties. Thai food.*

wine style: FRESH WHITE

WINZER KREMS 08 GRÜNER VELTLINER, AUSTRIA

589002 $10.75 UNDER $12

DOUBLE THE FUN WITH EVERYDAY BUBBLY

A morning latte to get through the workday, and a glass of sparkling in the evening to help unwind. You've heard it from Dr. Bill.

Too many people avoid sparkling wine because they think that the occasion doesn't warrant it. Which is a lot like waiting till your friends are dead to say how much you love 'em. Do it now. Not the entire bottle – just a glass a day – to celebrate the day. Refrigerated, open sparkling wine keeps well for 4 to 5 days. The two great everyday sparkling wines are Prosecco from Italy and Cava from Spain. And the good news is the LCBO offers excellent examples of both.

POST WORK WITH PROSECCO
Val d'Oca Prosecco delivers wonderful mineral zest and refreshment – dancing between purity and drinkability. An everyday bubbly that's sure to liven up your after work mood. A consistent best-in-class for over a decade.

Colio's Lily is a fresh, frank local sparkler in the Prosecco style. Won't have you seeing stars but will get your evening off to a lively start.

A CAVA A DAY
Cava is the official term for sparkling wine from the Catalan region of Spain. They use the traditional Champagne method of second fermentation in the bottle so there's a yeasty tang which adds to the refreshing experience. Cava is very everyday and affordable. And Segura Viudas is one of the best value wines in the world. Period. It should be the first thing in your shopping cart.

BEST TIMES: *Get over the sparkling fear – do it every day. And twice on the weekend. Check it out with sushi.*

*TIP!
Buy a good Champagne stopper to recork your bubbly and it will stay fresh all week. Refrigerate, of course.*

Fr
FRESH WHITE

wine style: FRESH WHITE

VAL D'OCA 08 PROSECCO BRUT, VALDOBBIADENE, ITALY 340570 $16.30

wine style: FRESH WHITE

COLIO ESTATE CEV 08 SPARKLING 'LILY', VQA ONTARIO 509083 $16.45

wine style: FRESH WHITE

SEGURA VIUDAS BRUT, SPAIN 158493 $14.95

BLACK & WHITE ELEGANT

Non-oaked Chardonnay is enjoying a wave of popularity but do you know that it's not a new wine style? Parts of France have always crafted this grape in a fresh, pure style and most bistros still sell a ton of the two best known editions – Macon Blanc and Chablis. Almost every bistro meals starts with a bottle of one of these. The first glass gets the juices flowing and the next one washes down a seafood appetizer or some local specialty.

A million French people can't be all wrong, so why not take their lead? For the first timer I suggest the Macon-Lugny (Macon is the region and Lugny is a parish). It's Chardonnay in its purist form – mildy fruity, bright and fresh, with a casual elegant feeling. Well-mannered wine to start the evening.

William Fevre's Chablis is as pure as virgin snow. Feels drier than Macon – wine to put your palate on edge, sharpen it up and get it going. Some wines taste of fruit – Chablis tastes like stone. In wine lingo this is called minerality. Think elegance and premium price. Minerality cannot be mass produced.

BEST TIMES: *As your opening act when the mood is slightly formal.*

wine style: FRESH WHITE

WILLIAM FEVRE 07 CHABLIS 'CHAMPS ROYAUX', BURGUNDY, FRANCE

276436 $22.40

wine style: FRESH WHITE

BOUCHARD PERE & FILS 07 MACON-LUGNY, BURGUNDY, FRANCE

51573 $14.75

GRIGIO THE REFRESHER

Pinot Grigio leads a double life. Most of the time it's Mr. Nice Guy, a social sipper, but there's a side of the family that's more high energy, and more refreshing. Wine to kick-start the night or event.

The northeast of Italy is home to Grigio and the more northerly the vineyards, the more likely you are to meet the refreshing style. Mezzacorona, a high-tech winery situated in the foothills of the Alps, delivers a good example of this style. Edgy, exuberant and out to get you and your thirst. A wild one that might not be popular at lazy time parties.

Ontario is starting to produce Grigios in this refreshing style. Check out Creekside's livewire 08. Pure flavours and tons of refreshment. Perfect with oysters or as an aperitif.

BEST TIMES: *With appetizers, or whenever you're thirsty.*

wine style: FRESH WHITE

MEZZACORONA 08 PINOT GRIGIO, TRENTINO, ITALY

302380 $12.65

wine style: FRESH WHITE

CREEKSIDE 08 PINOT GRIGIO, VQA NIAGARA

83196 $13.75

LIGHTHEARTED & REALLY GOOD AT IT

This book is about matching wines and moods so expect to meet lots of styles. Such as the light-hearted. Something simple, but good. Which is often what we're in the mood for. Our energies and thoughts are elsewhere and all we want from the wine is company. A little refreshment and a little pleasantness can go a long way.

Big commercial wineries usually overdo niceness in their simple wines but Lindemans got it exactly right in their 09 Pinot Grigio. A perfect mix of zippy and pleasant. Wine for weekend or early evening sipping.

René Barbier from Spain offers a similar combo of zest, niceness and lightheartedness. Shades of Pinot Grigio. Really good everyday company.

BEST TIMES: *Chillin' out, receptions, showers.*

wine style: FRESH WHITE UNDER $12

LINDEMANS 09 PINOT GRIGIO 'BIN 85', AUSTRALIA
668947 $10.95

wine style: FRESH WHITE UNDER $12

RENÉ BARBIER 08, PENEDES, SPAIN 332767 $9.75

Q: WHAT DO YOU MEAN BY BEST?

A: A best wine is one that works for the mood and situation. It all starts with the situation. There is no such thing as a BEST wine until you establish a context. Every wine in this book is offered with a mood or situation – a context – where the wine will BE best. Out of that context the wine is no longer a BEST. Got that? If not, you'll miss the whole point of this book.

Q: HOW DO YOU MAKE YOUR PICKS?

A: Good wine is a lot about the quality of the delivery. Therefore, I select wines that deliver a good edition of what they appear to be offering. For example, does the FRESH wine feel clear or muddled? Does the NICE & EASY white feel genuine or contrived? Does the RICH red feel interesting or just mellow? The better the delivery, the better it will satisfy the mood.

Q: DO YOU ACTUALLY TASTE ALL THE WINES IN THE STORES?

A: Absolutely. One bottle of each and in some cases, several. To write this book, I tasted well over 1,500 bottles. I wouldn't feel comfortable saying a wine was the 'best' unless I tasted all the competition. I think I can honestly say that I've had several glasses of every wine in this book. I'm not just a taster, I'm a drinker too.

FYI. Typically wine competitions only judge wines that are submitted. The award-winning wines are simply the best of what was entered. They are not necessarily the best of what's out there.

DID I SAY DRY?

If Dry and Riesling is still a novel concept for you, here are the wines to get you on track. However, if you've ever been told that you have a timid palate, you may want to skip this page.

Dry Riesling is the wine equivalent of a winter walk by the ocean in Newfoundland, or pushing the limits in a sports car – going out on an edge. A way of invigorating the senses and a way of making what comes after feel beautifully comforting.

The seriously dry feeling in Vineland and Sparr Rieslings is partly due to a mineral, stony coldness along with sharp acidity and the absence of much flavour. There is no better thirstquencher, aperitif, oyster or sushi wine. Especially during the summer. At ten percent alcohol it can be guzzled. But the extreme dryness is best appreciated in single glasses – spread the bottle over a few nights.

BEST TIMES: *For a jolt, a lift and refreshing the senses.*

wine style: FRESH WHITE

VINELAND ESTATES 07 DRY RIESLING, VQA NIAGARA
167551 $13.75

wine style: FRESH WHITE

PIERRE SPARR 08 RIESLING 'EXTREME', ALSACE, FRANCE 618546 $14.80

TIP: Look for the following premium Dry Rieslings on your Niagara visits:
THIRTY BENCH, CAVE SPRING, FLAT ROCK, TAWSE & HENRY OF PELHAM

FRESH & FUN

Ask Aussie winemakers what they like to drink and usually the answer is Riesling. "It's so damn refreshing."

To get a sense of what style of wine they're drinking I suggest you try a bottle of the wine below. It's not only refreshing but damn tasty too. Something I'd certainly want on my dessert island.

Australia brings an extra shot of flavour to the world of Dry Riesling, so the experience is full as well as zesty. It's the VW Beetle of the white wine world. A yellow one, of course.

***BEST TIMES:** To start your day, your party, or your new love affair. Good crowd-pleasing choice for family events, holiday festivities and a must for the beach.*

wine style: FRESH WHITE
WOLF BLASS 08 RIESLING 'YELLOW LABEL', AUSTRALIA 505370 $14.75

TAKE A WALK ON THE WILD SIDE

Sauvignon Blanc is the loud one, the rocker of the white wine world. It's the brass band at the head of the parade. It gets things started.

As with most things extreme, Sauv has lovers and haters. But I find that it works for everyone if you get the timing and mood correct. Such as at the cocktail hour. You would never pour Sauv late at night when people want comfort.

Sauvignon's refreshing nature is partly due to its herbaceous flavours which create a spa feeling. If the wine were a colour it would certainly be green. Lime green. It's no surprise that the most dramatic editions come from cool climate places such as New Zealand. One of their best and most consistent examples is Villa Maria – zesty, enthusiastic and raring to go.

BEST TIMES: *Aperitif and partner for seafood or soft cheeses such as goat. Best in summer of course.*

wine style: FRESH WHITE

VILLA MARIA 09 SAUVIGNON BLANC, MARLBOROUGH, NEW ZEALAND

426601 $15.95

ANOTHER WALK ON THE WILD SIDE

Ready for another injection of Sauvignon? While New Zealand is certainly top dog with this grape, other countries can also hit the high notes. Often for a few dollars less.

Santa Rita in Chile scores for exuberance and for value. And for consistency – it's been in my books for over a decade. Whereas purity is the hallmark of the Kiwi wines, this is a little earthy and richer. Shades of an old rocker. A must try for Stones fans!

Riscal's Rueda is produced from the Verdejo grape which is very Sauvignon-like. A wild one from Spain. Assertive, herbaceous and great for the cocktail hour. This wine has also been a model of consistency. Wish all Fresh Whites were in clear glass and screw cap.

BEST TIMES: *First glass for aperitif and the second with BBQ'd shrimp. But don't go all evening with these wild cats.*

wine style: FRESH WHITE

SANTA RITA 08 SAUVIGNON BLANC RESERVA, CHILE
275677 $13.95

wine style: FRESH WHITE

MARQUES DE RISCAL 08 RUEDA, SPAIN 36822 $12.15

SOFT ROCK SAUVINGONS

Not all Sauvs are headbangers. Some are crafted in an easy drinking style, with a notch or two less volume. Or to be more accurate, the high notes are tempered with pleasant fruitiness – making the wine more general purpose.

The Fetzer winery in California is a master at combining character and drinkability. And value. My kind of winery. Their Sauv is the perfect house wine for those who like it on the fresh side.

Jackson-Triggs also has a way of getting freshness and flavour to harmonize into a lively, happy feeling. Get it going with J-T.

wine style: FRESH WHITE

FETZER 08 SAUVIGNON BLANC 'VALLEY OAKS', CALIFORNIA 34033 $12.45

Every time I have Stoneleigh Sauv I ask myself why I don't buy it more often. Probably because it's a tad expensive for every day. But the show never fails to entertain. Energetic and fun. Beach Boys and the surfing scene. Would be an excellent intro to this grape variety.

Fr
FRESH WHITE

BEST TIMES: *To start the evening or party.*

wine style: FRESH WHITE

JACKSON-TRIGGS 08 SAUVIGNON BLANC, VQA NIAGARA 58438 $13.75

wine style: FRESH WHITE

STONELEIGH 08 SAUVIGNON BLANC, MARLBOROUGH, NEW ZEALAND

293043 $16.95

RETRO REFRESHERS

Here's a pair of whites that were high on the charts in the pre-Chard era. But simpler, more refreshing whites are making a comeback so maybe you'd like to explore Muscadet and Aligote.

Muscadet features frank freshness and a cool day feeling. It teases the palate and opens the door for things to follow. It's the intro to the event, the warm-up band. Wine for those who have the patience for foreplay. Add a dozen oysters and you have one of the world's greatest starter courses.

Aligote is another simple, northern France white that's traditionally served at the beginning of a meal. The Bosc family at Chateau des Charmes are producing a Niagara edition that's very close to the style of the original. A shade gentler and more flavourful than Muscadet. Aperitif or lunch wine. An undiscovered local star.

BEST TIMES: *Must be the first of the evening. Aperitif, or to partner with oysters or sushi.*

UNDER $12

wine style: FRESH WHITE
SAUVION 08 MUSCADET, LOIRE, FRANCE *143016 $10.40*

wine style: FRESH WHITE
CH. DES CHARMES 08 ALIGOTÉ, VQA NIAGARA-ON-THE-LAKE
284950 $13.25

START THE PARTY

Brut is the international designation for sparkling wines in the bone-dry style. But not all Bruts are the same. Some are friendly – party or anytime drinks.

Wolf Blass is a master at creating wines with great drinkability and his bubbly has the just-right feeling for parties and celebrations. Refreshingly crisp with lovely delicate flavours. French styling with the Aussie sense of fun. Good stuff.

Fr
FRESH WHITE

We met a bone-dry Prosecco earlier, now it's time for an easy drinking edition. The Bottega wine is not only crowd-pleasing but is also gutsy enough to partner with appetizers. Add a splash of Bottega Grappa (478156 $29.10) for a budget version of the classic champagne cocktail.

BEST TIMES: *Starting the party.*

wine style: FRESH SPARKLING

WOLF BLASS BRUT 'YELLOW LABEL', AUSTRALIA

649996 $17.95

wine style: FRESH SPARKLING

BOTTEGA PROSECCO 'VINO DEI POETI', ITALY

897702 $14.10

THE MOMENT FOR CHAMPAGNE

Champagne can be likened to religion – the more you believe, the more you get out of it. It's part drink, part imagination: the better your imagination; the better it works.

Champagne is quite austere and not really a fun, fun drink, if you know what I mean. But I love the delicacy, the purity, the refreshing tingle, the experience – and how it marks and celebrates a moment.

These are my favourite Champagnes picks: Piper-Heidsieck and Nicolas Feuillatte for their refreshing and delicate feeling. Lovely aperitif. Pol Roger for elegance and charm. Mumm `Carte Classique´ for the sugestion of sweetness and romance. And when Arsenal wins big games I pour the rich and exotic Louis Roederer.

***BEST TIMES:** When times are good, or really bad. (But don't go too long without Champagne.)*

wine style: FRESH SPARKLING

NICOLAS FEUILLATTE BRUT CHAMPAGNE, FRANCE

537605 $49.95

wine style: FRESH SPARKLING

PIPER-HEIDSIECK BRUT CHAMPAGNE, FRANCE

462432 $49.95

wine style: FRESH SPARKLING

MUMM 'CARTE CLASSIQUE', CHAMPAGNE, FRANCE
308064 $53.95c

wine style: FRESH SPARKLING

POL ROGER BRUT CHAMPAGNE, FRANCE 51953 $59.60

VE * Vintages Essentials
- always available

wine style: FRESH SPARKLING

LOUIS ROEDERER BRUT CHAMPAGNE, FRANCE 268771 VE $67.95

CHAMPAGNE-STYLE CELEBRATING FOR A FEW DOLLARS LESS

How much to pay for Sparkling has always been a wine drinker's dilemma. To Champagne or not?

The good news is that most of the world's wine regions now produce very good editions of sparkling wine. Champagne alternatives for sure.

Niagara's cool climate and soil structure are ideal for producing classic-style Sparkling. Such as Ch. des Charmes which has the high-pitched note and pure quality of Champagne. Quality bubbly.

Henry's Brut Rosé is a mix of challenging austerity and delicate flavours. Refreshing, stimulating and inspiring the imagination. Perfect.

Despite its hot climate, California produces very elegant Sparkling wines. Mumm Napa combines tart refreshment with sourdough flavours that create a hugh desire for food. Topnotch aperitif.

BEST TIMES: *Events that call for something special.*

wine style: FRESH SPARKLING

CHATEAU DES CHARMES BRUT, VQA NIAGARA-ON-THE-LAKE

145409 $22.95

wine style: FRESH SPARKLING

MUMM NAPA BRUT 'PRESTIGE', CALIFORNIA

265678 $27.75

wine style: FRESH SPARKLING

HENRY OF PELHAM BRUT ROSÉ 'CUVEE CATHARINE', VQA NIAGARA

4051 $29.75

Ne
NICE & EASY

COMFORTABLE
MEDIUM ENERGY
NO WORRIES
SOCIAL
EVERYDAY
GENTLE & POLITE
ALONE OR WITH FRIENDS
POLITICALLY CORRECT
OPEN HOUSE/ WEDDING RECEPTIONS

NICE & EASY WHITES

SITTING PRETTY

Typically, Viognier could be likened to Chardonnay's younger cousin. Every bit as pretty but more modest. Not yet wearing or needing makeup. The grape originated in the south of France and has only recently started to travel.

Chile's Cono Sur winery produces some of the best tasting, value priced wines in the world. I don't know how they do it but some of their offerings can rival wines at twice the price. Their Viognier, for example.

But don't expect a lot of modesty – this is a charmer. A young princess, an innocent seductress. Lovely combination of pretty flavours and citrus freshness. Hard to imagine a more delightful house wine.

BEST TIMES: *Anytime sipping.*

FYI: The Cono Sur name is a play on words – the southern cone (the ice cream cone shape of South America) and the French word connoisseur. The winery's motto is `no boring history or dusty cellars'. The bike logo reflects the winery's environmentally-friendly practices.

wine style: NICE & EASY WHITE

CONO SUR 08 VIOGNIER, CHILE 64287 $9.75

UNDER $12

CHEAP 'N CHEERFUL

Yes, you can still buy good everyday white wine for a lot less than ten bucks. If you have never tried the following pair you're in for a surprise, and some savings.

How can cheap wine be any good? The wines below come from large wineries with a lot of clout when it comes to buying grapes, and that can afford small margins because of huge sales. The Costco model. The bright, fresh character is a product of skilled winemaking and modern technology.

KWV's Chenin offers a little zest, a little fruitiness and a lot of easy drinkability. So simple but so agreeable. A world champ in the everyday wine category.

The Chardonnay also combines pleasantness and simplicity. It's non-oaked and refreshing. Wine to partner life's quiet times. Both wines have moderate alcohol levels.

BEST TIMES: *Daytime drinking, lunch, early evening, weekend sipping, friends on the porch, big family events.*

wine style: NICE & EASY WHITE

KWV 09 CHENIN BLANC, SOUTH AFRICA 18689 $7.75 UNDER $12

wine style: NICE & EASY WHITE

CESARI 08 CHARDONNAY, VENEZIE, ITALY 572461 $7.45 UNDER $12

TWITTER WORTHY

Magazines are always telling us about hot wines but some of the best get overlooked. Such as the following pair. Whites worth a tweet or two.

Orvieto ruled the Italian white section in the pre-Grigio era and it looks like Ruffino is out to regain some of that territory with its delicious 08 vintage. Lively, fruity and dishing out the charm. Super-nice, super-good and lots of fun for the price. Too bad the label wasn't upgraded along with the wine.

La Vieille Ferme is an everyday, South of France white that's well above average because it's made by the Perrin bros who own the prestigious Ch. de Beaucastel in Chateauneuf du Pape. Crisp and fruity, and I'd give it ten out of ten on the nice scale.

BEST TIMES: *House whites that can handle most lighter foods.*

wine style: NICE & EASY WHITE

UNDER $12

RUFFINO 08 ORVIETO, UMBRIA, ITALY 31062 $11.50

wine style: NICE & EASY WHITE

UNDER $12

LA VIEILLE FERME 08 CÔTES DU LUBERON, FRANCE 298505 $11.65

PARTY-ON DUDE

Gallo didn't become the largest winery in the world without knowing a thing or two about popular taste. They make wines that people like. Such as the newly arrived Barefoot Bubbly.

The Barefoot brand is designed for a young audience looking for less wine lore and more friendliness. And what could be friendlier than a wine called Bubbly that's made from Pinot Grigio. Perfect for the casual life suggested by the Barefoot name and logo.

As you might expect this is not a bone-dry sparkling wine. Fruit flavours and easy drinking are the features. But there is a hit of refreshment and it's not too cute – just right for pleasing most guests at your next party, especially in the early stages.

BEST TIMES: *Everyday bubbly to please lots of ages and tastes. Perfect for weddings and family bashes.*

FYI:
BAREFOOT N/V PINOT GRIGIO (53983 $9.95) *is a tasty, lighthearted, gulp-me party wine. At a party price.*

wine style: NICE & EASY SPARKLING

BAREFOOT BUBBLY PINOT GRIGIO, CALIFORNIA
106088 $12.95

FOR THE LAZY DAYS OF SUMMER

Ontario produces one of the world's great summer wines – semi-dry Riesling. A drink that delivers tasty flavours, lots of zest and which is moderate in alcohol. The slight sweetness delivers the important 'let's relax' message. Lulls us into a contented state and connects us to summer.

The folks at Vineland and Cave Spring have been plying us with fantastic semi-dry Riesling for as long as I've been writing these books. `Girls Night Out´ is a new addition.

No other region produces this style of wine so it's both a great drink and a cause for Canadian celebration. Buy a bottle and take the day off.

Vineland's style is super-peppy and joyful. (Look for a new label shortly.) Cave's wine is gentler and more soothing. `Girls´ is a party crowd-pleaser. Take your pick.

BEST TIMES: *Summer afternoons or weekend brunches.*

wine style: NICE & EASY WHITE

VINELAND ESTATES 07 SEMI-DRY RIESLING, VQA NIAGARA 232033 $13.95

wine style: NICE & EASY WHITE

CAVE SPRING CELLARS 07 RIESLING, VQA NIAGARA 234583 $14.25

wine style: NICE & EASY WHITE

COLIO ESTATE 08 RIESLING 'GIRLS' NIGHT OUT', VQA LAKE ERIE NORTH SHORE 134917 $12.75

LOCAL NON-OAKED CHARDONNAY

In the previous Fresh White category, I told you about the two original non-oaked Chardonnays from France. Now it's time to explore some very good locals. Ontario is one of the few places outside France than can make this style.

For non-oaked Chard, you need a cool climate to achieve a good balance of vitality, fruitiness and purity. Wines with a vibrancy. Hot climate editions are too ripe and taste a lot like oaked Chardonnay.

Vineland's Chardonnay is not only a sleeper in the local section, but in the entire store. Simple on first impression, but it doesn't take long to notice its confidence. Chardonnay with a comfortable, take-me-anywhere feeling. Smart new label – but why not screw cap?

Pelee is also a bargain. A little refreshment and a whole lot of delicious frutiness. One hell of a nice drink.

One of the stars and values of the year in local wine is Hillebrand's Artist Series. Bright fruity flavours, a little creaminess and a genuinely nice personality. Very Canuk. Get on this before it sells out.

Pelham is a seasoned pro at this style and always gets the right mix of zest, tasty fruit and drinkability. Very crowd-pleasing.

BEST TIMES: *These are the t-shirt and blue jeans of wine – everyday comfort. Celebrate and shop local.*

wine style: NICE & EASY WHITE

VINELAND ESTATES 08 CHARDONNAY, VQA NIAGARA

69374 $12.65

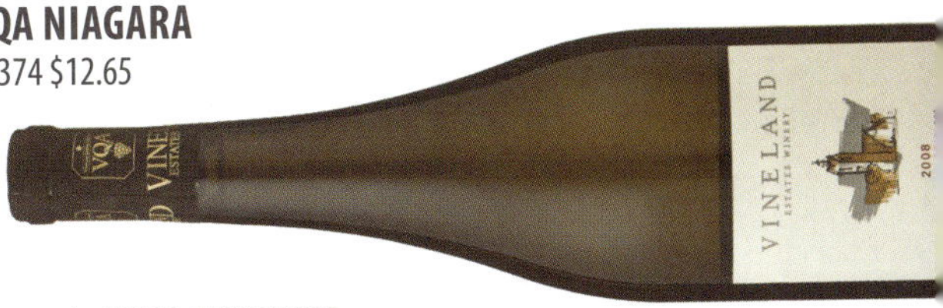

wine style: NICE & EASY WHITE

HILLEBRAND 08 UNOAKED CHARDONNAY 'ARTIST SERIES', VQA NIAGARA

83385 $10.95

UNDER $12

Ne
NICE & EASY WHITE

wine style: NICE & EASY WHITE

HENRY OF PELHAM 07 NON-OAKED CHARDONNAY, VQA NIAGARA

291211 $13.15

wine style: NICE & EASY WHITE

PELEE ISLAND 08 NON-OAKED CHARDONNAY, VQA ONTARIO

UNDER $12

136044 $10.75

SHOW-OFF CHARD

Chardonnay is a multi-personality wine. It can be anything from a classy dame to a sexy bombshell. Most of what's offered in stores reflects popular taste – a little sweet, overdressed, over perfumed and show-offish. Saturday night at the club. Fun times.

Inniskillin's wine is semi-rich, loaded with tropical fruit flavours and just dying to please. A local edition of the Aussie experience.

Stone Cellars wine reminds me of the first time I tasted Californian Chardonnay. A wow flavour experience. Fruit cocktail laced with tingling freshness. A summer day at the beach feeling. Not a bad trip for the price.

Prospect Winery also offers a yummy party drink. Lots of spicy/sweet flavours along with lemony zest. Drink on.

BEST TIMES: *Parties with lots of spicy and sweet BBQ'd foods.*

Ne
NICE & EASY WHITE

wine style: NICE & EASY WHITE

INNISKILLIN 08 CHARDONNAY 'VARIETAL SERIES', VQA ONTARIO 66266 $10.95 UNDER $12

wine style: NICE & EASY WHITE

BERINGER 08 CHARDONNAY 'STONE CELLARS', CALIFORNIA 606806 $13.65

wine style: NICE & EASY WHITE

PROSPECT WINERY 06 CHARDONNAY 'THE CENSUS COUNT', VQA OKANAGAN
92296 $14.95

Q: DO I NEED TO SPEND MORE TO GET MORE?

A: No way! This used to be the case but winemaking and viticulture have improved on parallel lines with techno toys. Good stuff now costs less. But what if you were to spend $50 or $100 – what would you experience? Sometimes more flavour, sometimes a richer wine, sometimes a more luxurious feeling. Often you're just paying for a brand name, as with cars or cosmetics. But in most cases you simply get a more polished, smoother wine. Most people equate smoothness with quality and are happy to pay a premium for it. Smooth is a close relative of boring.

Q: CAN I REALLY GET A GOOD WINE FOR UNDER $10?

A: Yes. And there's even good reds from Italy and Argentina for under $8. I can't believe how many people don't know this. Many of these bargains also come in a magnum size, which converts to about $6 a bottle! Go get 'em!

HAPPY FACED SAUVIGNONS

Sauvignon, like Chardonnay, comes with many faces. The name of the grape on the label can be helpful or misleading. That's why I don't use grape varieties as the basis for my categories.

Here's three Sauvignons bred for fun rather than wildness. They're super enjoyable because they hit the sweet spot between freshness and niceness.

Nederburg and Fish Hoek have a jazzy, happy feeling and would be a hit at any party. Gently refreshing and flavourful, but big on drinkability. Handy screw cap and friendly price. Check out my other recommendations from these wineries.

Caliterra's wine is also riding the pleasant trail. Delicious tropical fruit flavours, lots of zest and tons of good cheer. You'll not be short of friends with this in your fridge. Also screw-capped and well-priced.

BEST TIMES: *Anytime! Try Sauvignons with Thai curries and sushi.*

wine style: NICE & EASY WHITE

UNDER $12

NEDERBURG 08 SAUVIGNON BLANC 'WINEMASTER'S RESERVE', SOUTH AFRICA

283713 $10.95

Ne NICE & EASY WHITE

UNDER $12

wine style: NICE & EASY WHITE

CALITERRA 09 SAUVIGNON BLANC RESERVA, CHILE

275909 $8.95

UNDER $12

wine style: NICE & EASY WHITE

FISH HOEK 09 SAUVIGNON BLANC, SOUTH AFRICA

129726 $9.95

LIFE WITH GRIGIO

I spent a few days on the road with a friend who drank nothing but Pinot Grigio. We were in the States where every bar pours the stuff. Meanwhile, I wasted time and money looking for more interesting wine experiences. By day three I wised up and went with Grigio – because I'd learned a lesson.

Daytime and social drinking are not really about the drink, and are best served by something simple. We're on cruise control then – not building up to dinner. All we need is a pleasant, mildly refreshing wine – a friendship drink – such as Pinot Grigio.

Spinelli's wine might have a shade too much personality for an American bar, but that's why I like it. Grigio with character. Makes me wonder why we pay $13 for non-oaked Chardonnays! Pair it with Spinelli Sangiovese in my Rustic section.

Citra also delivers more bright flavours and refreshment than you might expect for the price. A sort of Joe Fresh experience.

BEST TIMES: *Daytime, hanging out on the patio and socializing in general. And in American bars.*

wine style: NICE & EASY WHITE

SPINELLI 08 PINOT GRIGIO, ABRUZZI, ITALY

113886 $8.95 UNDER $12

wine style: NICE & EASY WHITE

CITRA 08 PINOT GRIGIO, ABRUZZI, ITALY

17483 $7.95 UNDER $12

CROWD-PLEASING TEN-DOLLAR WHITES

Argentina, Chile and Italy are today's leaders in bargain-priced white wines. The South Americans deliver big flavours and a slight sweetness while Italy's style is drier and less flamboyant.

I think that Caliterra would win the `people's choice award´ in ten-dollar whites. It has the usual Chard line of exotic flavours and richness but the main statement is liveliness. It's bouncy, it's fun and it has a beat you could dance to. Let the party begin.

The 09 Vintage of Fuzion has the exotic flavours of hot climate Chards but is drier than most. And feels less contrived. There's an edge and a citrussy tang.

Mezzomondo rocked our world with budget reds and are set to do it again with this white. It's fruity, semi-rich and super-pleasant. Shades of non-oaked Chardonnay – at a discounted price.

Grillo is a native Sicilian grape producing wines with a mix of vitality and comfort. Very pleasant. Would be welcome at any party.

BEST TIMES: *Anytime!*

wine style: NICE & EASY WHITE

UNDER $12

CALITERRA 08 CHARDONNAY RESERVA, CHILE
257147 $8.95

UNDER $12

wine style: NICE & EASY WHITE

FAMILIA ZUCCARDI 09 CHENIN/CHARDONNAY 'FUZION', ARGENTINA 119800 $7.45

UNDER $12

wine style: NICE & EASY WHITE

MEZZOMONDO 08 PINOT GRIGIO/CHARDONNAY, SICILY 79301 $9.95

UNDER $12

wine style: NICE & EASY WHITE

ARANCIO 08 GRILLO, SICILY 114710 $11.75

Ne
NICE & EASY WHITE

A MERRY-GO-ROUND OF NICENESS

Here's a bunch of really nice wines with no special characteristics other than they would be popular on the party circuit. Not stars but you could do a lot worse.

Pinot Grigio has always been good from Pelee. Fruity, friendly and fun to relax with.

Lindemans Bin wines are all crowd-pleasers but I particularly like the low alcohol Sauv for hot weather gulping.

Alsace Pinot Blanc tastes a lot like non-oaked Chard – fruity and pretty. The producers name is a bit of a mouthful but the wine is easy.

wine style: NICE & EASY WHITE

PELEE ISLAND 08 PINOT GRIGIO, VQA ONTARIO UNDER $12

326413 $11.95

wine style: NICE & EASY WHITE

LINDEMANS 09 SAUVGINON BLANC 'BIN 95', AUSTRALIA UNDER $12

181388 $10.95

wine style: NICE & EASY WHITE

PFAFFENHEIM 07 PINOT BLANC, ALSACE, FRANCE

22855 $13.25

Beringer's wines can be overly sweet but it's hard not to like the fresh, fruity, ten-dollar Grigio. Excessive sweetness is often a trait in Yellow Tail wines too, but their PG has lovely lemony freshness. Adult lemonade.

Hardy's Hottage Hill Chard is refreshing, flavourful and playful. A good everyday drink.

BEST TIMES: *Relaxing alone or with friends. Pour for open houses.*

wine style: NICE & EASY WHITE

BERINGER 08 PINOT GRIGIO 'CALIFORNIA COLLECTION', CALIFORNIA

UNDER $12

112995 $9.95

wine style: NICE & EASY WHITE

YELLOW TAIL 09 PINOT GRIGIO, AUSTRALIA

UNDER $12

8254 $11.20

wine style: NICE & EASY WHITE

HARDYS 08 CHARDONNAY 'NOTTAGE HILL', AUSTRALIA

UNDER $12

238457 $11.25

THE BEAUTY OF THE BLEND

The Aussie's love their white blends such as Sem/ Sauv and Sem/Chard and now we're starting to see a similar practice from our local wineries. And why not, if it produces something different or better than single grape variety wines.

Malivoire's new blend of Chardonnay, Riesling and Gewurztraminer is super-pleasant. Manages to be both refreshing and pretty. The kiss of Gewurz in the blend adds charm and seduction. Would be a lot of people's idea of a really nice white wine. So here's your chance to win friends. Screw cap and stylish new label. An impressive first-at-the-LCBO for Malivoire.

Inniskillin is using the same blend with somewhat similar results. A wine alive with pretty flavours and tingling freshness – comfy richness too. Feels like a Cirque de Soleil experience.

Coyote's Run is less flamboyant. Everyday but wonderful, like buying a new pair of jeans. Another sure to please wine. Screw cap and clear glass bottle add a bright, modern touch.

BEST TIMES: *Fun wines for whenever.*

wine style: NICE & EASY WHITE
MALIVOIRE 08 WHITE, VQA NIAGARA
141531 $14.95

wine style: NICE & EASY WHITE
INNISKILLIN 08 'BRAE BLANC' GEWURZTRAMINER, CHARDONNAY, RIESLING, VQA NIAGARA
109975 $14.75

wine style: NICE & EASY WHITE
COYOTE'S RUN 08 PINOT GRIS/PINOT BLANC, VQA ONTARIO
112144 $15.75

Ri

RICH

COMFORTING
SEDUCTIVE
ROMANTIC
SUBSTANTIAL
CLASSICAL
SPECIAL EVENTS
SLOW
LINGERING
IMPRESSIVE
LOW ENERGY
LAYERED & RICH

RICH WHITES

WORTH DRESSING UP FOR

These are kinda special. Only borderline rich but feeling more elegant than most of the wines in this section. You could cover a lot of bases with either, especially if you give them a little formality and attention.

Masianco and San Vincenzo are part of a new breed of Italian white wines that are competing with the international grape varieties by elevating the quality of traditional Italian grapes. I say bravo and hope you'll join me in supporting their efforts to maintain diversity in wine.

Masi has enriched Pinot Grigio by adding partially dried Verduzzo grapes – borrowing a little from the region's famous red, Amarone. Richness is partnered with mineral coolness and a little mystery. Feels very Mediterranean.

Anselmi's wine is a premium Soave but marketed with a brand name to distance itself from Soave's lowly image. It's a shade prettier than the Masianco. Feels upscale. Pour it for your date.

Both wines hit a middle ground between my Fresh and Rich categories. While the flavours are modest, you can feel the richness – but the main feature is elegance, and a gradual unfolding over the course of the bottle.

BEST TIMES: *Dinner parties. One glass for an aperitif will set the tone after which seafood appetizers, linguine alfredo or roast chicken are possible food partners.*

Ri
RICH WHITE

wine style: RICH WHITE

MASI 08 'MASIANCO' PINOT GRIGIO/VERDUZZO, VENETO, ITALY

620773 $14.95

wine style: RICH WHITE

ANSELMI 08 'SAN VINCENZO', VENETO, ITALY

948158 VE $16.95

EAST MEETS WEST

Ontario is conservative and the West Coast is hip and sexy. So they say. And there are wines to prove the point!

Chateau des Charmes Estate Chardonnay is very composed, very together. The flavours are hushed, the richness is under raps – the feeling is quiet but confident. No hurry to impress, that happens later in the bottle. Politeness rules. Even the beautiful new label is understated.

The Okanagen Valley produces extroverted wines with exotic flavours. Lush and charming. Nothing held back. Jackson-Triggs Sauvignon has the zesty spirit of the grape but it's mainly about seduction.

BEST TIMES: *An East/West party.*

wine style: RICH WHITE
CHATEAU DES CHARMES 07 ESTATE CHARDONNAY, VQA NIAGARA-ON-THE-LAKE 81653 $13.95

wine style: RICH WHITE
JACKSON-TRIGGS 07 SAUVIGNON BLANC, VQA OKANAGAN VALLEY 593111 $13.75

TASTE THE ORIGINAL CHARDONNAY

Burgundy is the ancestral home of Chardonnay. And of the practice of ageing it in oak casks. Many years ago I bought a case of Jadot's white Burgundy because I was intrigued by what at the time I called its whiskey flavour. Turned out I wasn't imagining things – Burgundy and whiskey are aged in similar barrels.

The oak cask ageing ads a little spicy sweetness to wine and it also can make a white wine feel more earthy, solid, and in Jadot's case, more masculine. Down 'n dirty. All of which increases the wine's ability to partner with food, especially with well-seasoned food. White Burgundy is similar to New World Chards but is a shade drier and more refreshing – tighter engineering.

BEST TIMES: *Well-seasoned BBQ'd white meats for an exciting meeting of macho and macho.*

wine style: RICH WHITE

LOUIS JADOT 07 CHARDONNAY, BURGUNDY, FRANCE

733077 VE $20.95

VE* Vintages Essentials - always available

THE CALIFORNIA GANG

While the last decade was all about Australia let me remind you that it was California that converted most North Americans to wine. And it was Chardonnay that did it. I was smitten even though I came from the European school.

California lost market share when it became expensive – they started pricing like the high-end French regions. Australia stepped in and offered better value, but today Chile is under selling the Aussies. So where does that leave California? Back in the market, with wines that deliver quality when you're in the mood for premium.

Mondavi 'Private Selection' is one of the best lines of premium wines available. Most are recommended in this book. The Chardonnay is a good mix of glamour and elegance. Pretty stuff wearing a stylish Oscar night outfit. Dinner party wine for sure.

You'll find a little more flavour concentration in J. Lohr. Super-rich, exotic flavours gush in all directions. Lots to like. There's a firmness too so it partners really well with BBQ'd foods.

The folks at Sonoma-Cutrer aim for a Franco-American style Chard. Flavourful but not over-the-top. A sleek sports car feeling – a bracing ride to your Hollywood mansion. Good with rich seafood because of the refreshing qualities. A must for fancy dinner parties.

BEST TIMES: *Dinner parties with BBQ'd white meats or seafood. Hot and spicy seasonings plays nicely with the slight sweetness in the wine.*

wine style: RICH WHITE
ROBERT MONDAVI 07 CHARDONNAY 'PRIVATE SELECTION', CALIFORNIA 379180 $17.95

wine style: RICH WHITE
J. LOHR 07 CHARDONNAY 'RIVERSTONE', CALIFORNIA 258699 $19.95

wine style: RICH WHITE
SONOMA-CUTRER 07 CHARDONNAY, RUSSIAN RIVER RANCHES, CALIFORNIA 608653 VE $24.95

VE* Vintages Essentials - always available

Q: ARE WE WELL-SERVED BY A MONOPOLY?

A: Yes and no. Yes, because a monopoly gives people outside the big cities a relatively good selection of drinks. No, because it controls everything – the wine choices, the prices and the 'flavour' of the industry. And it robs us of tons of interesting and obscure wines that can only be handled by private enterprise stores. The LCBO can be likened to the big supermarkets – they are good at a lot of things, they try really hard to be your friend – but in the end the stores are still soulless boxes. I'd like to see the Nova Scotia model where government stores supply the everyday, and private stores offer the interesting.

Q: SHOULD I TAKE A WINE COURSE?

A: You could and you might enjoy it. But I've found that once you cross the line into wine 'learning', things happen that interfere with pure wine enjoyment. Your focus shifts to details, information and matters of the head. The heart gets pushed back and that's not good because wine is about PLEASURE and it's the heart that rules PLEASURE. I've found that if you pay attention, wine will teach you. But do familiarize yourself with names of regions and grapes.

ALL DAY CHARD

Wyndham is best known for their `Bin 555´ Shiraz, but don't overlook their Chardonnay. I did, till a recent winemaker's lunch where it was poured as the aperitif. How crass I thought, pouring a rich Chard at eleven in the morning! Ten minutes later my mind was changed.

Sure, there's lots of flashy, tropical fruit flavours in `Bin 222´, but the heart and soul of this wine is zestiness. A bright, alive, and cheerful feeling – all the qualities you want in a mid-morning wine. The richness catches up with you later and when it's time for the shrimp, the jerk chicken, the creamy pasta…or whatever is going.

BEST TIMES: *A wine to take you through the entire day.*

wine style: RICH WHITE

WYNDHAM ESTATES
07 CHARDONNAY
'BIN 222', AUSTRALIA

93401 $12.45

THE RICH FEELING AT AN EVERYDAY PRICE

If you enjoy the richness of Chardonnay you need to know about this pair of Chilean wonders. Two of the best Chardonnay buys in the world.

Carmen Chardonnay is the street corner Rolex – a deal for sure. Would embarrass a lot of Chards at three times the price. My favourite deep, earthy flavours coupled with citrussy freshness. Richness partnered with liveliness. Love that combo.

If manly is more your style, grab the Santa Rita. Rich wine with a bold tang. Chard for BBQ'd flavours. Tangy is a good feature as it refreshes and balances the richness in both the wine and the food.

Ri
RICH WHITE

BEST TIMES: *Looking for a big bang for your buck.*

wine style: RICH WHITE

CARMEN 08 CHARDONNAY, CHILE 235663 $9.70

UNDER $12

wine style: RICH WHITE

SANTA RITA 07 CHARDONNAY RESERVA, CHILE

348359 $13.95

BIG BOLD CANADIANS

Super-rich wines aren't really the Canadian way, but it's interesting to see it can be done. Usually in small quantities and sold at source. However, the following are out there when you need a hit of rich white.

Le Clos Jordanne comes in a range of styles and prices but I'm favouring the least expensive offering for best overall value. Crafted in the Burgundian style, it's bold, masculine and quite dry. Forget Chardonnay glamour – this guy is a cutting edge partner for rich foods, and has deep earthy flavours to hold your interest till the final drop. Available at Wine Rack stores.

The hot, desert-like climate of the Okanagan Valley is well-suited for producing rich wines with bold ripe flavours. Mission Hill's Chard is starting to develop a mellow feeling. Couch sipping.

BEST TIMES: *A semi-formal mood and grilled white meats.*

wine style: RICH WHITE

LE CLOS JORDANNE 06 CHARDONNAY, VILLAGE RESERVE, VQA NIAGARA Wine Rack stores $25.00

wine style: RICH WHITE

MISSION HILL 06 CHARDONNAY RESERVE, VQA OKANAGAN, B.C. 545004 VE $19.95

CHARD FOR THE BARBEE

OK mates, we're getting down and dirty on the Barbee – chicken thighs, corn and potatoes – so forget all those sissy Grigios and Rieslings. We need big, bold, manly Chard. Boozy, sweaty stuff from Australia of course. Something to handle foods smothered with kickass spices – a wine that's up for the challenge. Bring it on.

Cookoothama may not be the biggest hit of Aussie Chard but it delivers lots for the price. And it gets the job done with charred foods.

BEST TIMES: *The BBQ season.*

wine style: RICH WHITE

NUGAN ESTATE 07 CHARDONNAY 'COOKOOTHAMA', AUSTRALIA

619403 $13.95

STRATUS WINERY, NIAGARA-ON-THE-LAKE

TRY SOMETHING ELSE

There was a time when Alsace wines were high on the charts. Then along came the Chardonnay/ Sauvignon era. Not having these grapes in their portfolio, Alsace was hit hard.

But Alsace has a savior wine – Pinot Gris. Same thing as Pinot Grigio, but bred and crafted in a richer style. An alternative to Chardonnay. Unique in that's it's one of the few rich wines in the world that's is not oak-aged. A natural beauty!

Leon Beyer has been a regular in my books and the 07 vintage is up to form. On the lighter side of rich, with delicate flavours, a little spiciness and lots of zest. Very composed and elegant.

I've been tasting lots of Sicilian whites over the past few years – they have something going on that's a little different. High elevation vineyards are producing whites with a lovely mix of freshness, delicacy and richness. Montalto's wine is Pinot Grigio with substance. Manages to feel both every-day and a bit special. Good before and with dinner.

BEST TIMES: *Try these with charcuterie, baked ham or grilled fish.*

wine style: RICH WHITE

LEON BEYER 07 PINOT GRIS, ALSACE, FRANCE

165241 $15.95

wine style: RICH WHITE

BARONE MONTALTO 08 PINOT GRIGIO, SICILY UNDER $12

731148 $9.95

Li

LIVELY

GULPABLE
SPORTY
MEDIUM-HIGH
ENERGY
LIGHTLY CHILLED
VITALITY
ALFRESCO LUNCHES
PICNICS
CAFÉ & BISTRO REDS
TART
FUN TIMES

LIVELY
REDS

THINK PINK – DRY ROSÉ

I'm delighted to see that pink wine is at last catching on. Even with the guys. My Men in Pink lunch was a big hit this summer.

The trick to enjoying pink is to pick up on the wine's invitation to have fun. Lighten up, for God's sake. When the sun is shining and you want to be outdoors, pink is the way to go.

We're talking dry Rosé here, refreshment as well as fun, and of course, served chilled as you do with whites. But you also get some of the flavour characteristics of red wine, especially when the Rosé warms up on the table.

Besides the summer, dry Rosé works well on holidays such as Thanksgiving and Christmas. It partners well with all kinds of food and the colour complements the festive spirit. Rosé with Indian curry is one of my favourite wine and food combinations.

I'd like to congratulate the LCBO on the huge array of dry Rosé offered each summer. These are one-shot purchases and for recommendations read my blog (www.billysbestbottles.com) in June and July. The following are always available.

Lamberti Chiaretto has been a good staple house Rosé for over a decade. Delicate in flavour and feeling, but with enough refreshment to liven the palate. Very summer patio-ish.

For a richer, supper table Rosé, check out the new kid from Ventoux in the South of France. Tasty fruit

FYI: Blush is also pink but quite sweet. A wine crafted for people who enjoy fruit-flavoured drinks.

flavours along with a little earthiness. Very bistro and very good value.

Jackson-Triggs produces a berry flavour Rosé with a touch of sweetness. A good party drink or partner for spicy hot foods.

BEST TIMES: *The summer months and family events. Partner dry Rosé with Indian curry, paella, charcuterie or bouillabaisse.*

wine style: DRY ROSÉ
LAMBERTI 08 BARDOLINO CHIARETTO 'SANTEPIETRE', VENETO, ITALY 396572 $11.25 UNDER $12

wine style: DRY ROSÉ
OGIER 08 ROSÉ VENTOUX, RHÔNE, FRANCE UNDER $12
134916 $11.95

wine style: DRY ROSÉ
JACKSON-TRIGGS 08 CABERNET FRANC ROSÉ, VQA NIAGARA 79467 $13.95

EXPLORING THE BACK ROADS WITH GAMAY

These days there's often little difference between most reds, so if you want variety and adventure, you need to take some detours.

One of the joys of drinking less popular wines is nobody is telling you what to enjoy. On the back-road trip you are free to make your own discoveries – the guide books haven't gone there.

Gamay is my favourite backroads local. It's the grape of Beaujolais but there's little family resemblance in the Ontario kids. Our Gamays have more of an Italian personality – gutsy and earthy. Honest everyday wine. Shades of the light tart reds found in the cafes of Europe. I think it would help sales if wineries used clear glass bottles to deliver the message of the wine's light, lively style.

Angels Gate wine is lively – the playful daytime spirit. Forget smoothness, this red has white wine zest and refreshment. Lightly chill and let the games begin.

Chateau des Charmes white label is always one of Niagara's best light reds. Fruity with a refreshing, peppery kick. Lightly chill, decant out of the boring bottle and be prepared for a fun and fast ride.

Prince Edward County is getting into the Gamay game with a vibrant, gutsy, very Italian wine from the Grange winery.

BEST TIMES: *Daytime or early evening. Lightly chill.*

TIP: Look for the following premium Gamays on your Niagara visits:

PELLER ESTATES 07 GAMAY 'PRIVATE RESERVE' $18.00

MALIVOIRE ESTATES 07 GAMAY $18.00

13th STREET WINERY 07 GAMAY $18.00

STRATUS 07 GAMAY $28.00

wine style: LIVELY RED

ANGELS GATE 07 GAMAY, VQA NIAGARA

107714 $12.95

wine style: LIVELY RED

CH. DES CHARMES 07 GAMAY 'WHITE LABEL' VQA ONTARIO 57349 $12.45

wine style: LIVELY RED

THE GRANGE 07 GAMAY 'TRUMPOUR'S MILL', VQA PRINCE EDWARD COUNTY

615062 $14.80

DEBORAH PASKUS winemaker at Closson Chase winery, Prince Edward County

Q: IS THERE A SIMPLE FORMULA FOR MATCHING FOOD AND WINE?

A: Yep. The food you select (at home or in a restaurant) will reflect your mood and needs. Pay attention to what you're in the mood for – and that will tell you what style of wine you need. For instance, the desire to have steak suggests the need for nourishment, therefore the wine should be nourishing too…a RICH red. If you're in the mood for pizza, then match this playful, casual food with a similar wine…such as a LIVELY Valpolicella. If you're in the mood for sushi, then you're wanting bright, clean flavours…you want a FRESH Dry Riesling. Tune in to the mood and spirit of the food and you'll find its mate. You're always choosing wine for the situation rather than the food. This might be one of the most important things you'll read in this book. It's rule #1. I'll repeat it: don't choose wine for food – choose wine for the event.

Q: WHY YOU DON'T TALK ABOUT THE COMPONENTS IN WINE SUCH AS TANNINS, ACIDS AND FLAVOURS?

A: I concentrate on the feeling instead. Wine drinking is not really about the wine but the experience one has with it. The stuff happening to you. Wine geeks talk about flavours – hints of this and that – but for me wines deliver an impact, a feeling that's bigger than all the singular components. The communication between people and wine is based on that feeling. If you're just cataloguing flavours or long finishes and tannins, you can't get to the heart of the wine. Wine works a lot like music. We respond to the feelings it evokes, not just the notes and instruments. Think about how we connect to different styles of music and it will help you understand wine.

BAGUETTE, BRIE & BEAUJOLAIS

Add a bouquet of balloons to a picnic table and you have a very good image of the Beaujolais experience. The wine to accompany fun, lighthearted times.

Beaujolais' liveliness, fruitiness and moderate alcohol is the perfect recipe for summer drinking. And it's one of the few red wines that is thirst-quenching – providing you lightly chill it. Too bad the arrival of Beaujolais Nouveau in November gets people thinking it's a winter drink. It's not. Drink it in the summer.

I find that Beaujolais also hits the spot at festive times to introduce fun, and to balance the heavy foods. I always pour it on Thanksgiving and Christmas afternoons.

The quality of Beaujolais is excellent in the 08 vintage. And prices have barely increased in a decade, so it's one of today's wine bargains.

Mommessin's wine is an exuberant mix of tartness and freshness. White wine in a red wine cloak. Delicious refreshment for an alfresco lunch. Mommessin is much improved from the old days.

Duboeuf's wine also has the fruity/tart thing happening. Mouth puckering refreshment. Bread and cheese never tasted so good.

The invitation to play is perfectly captured in Bouchard's wine. Yummy flavours with spring day freshness.

P. S. You'll meet more Beaujolais is the Rustic section.

BEST TIMES: *Outdoors in the summer, or anytime when the mood is lighthearted.*

wine style: LIVELY RED
MOMMESSIN 08 BEAUJOLAIS, FRANCE 313734 $11.25 UNDER $12

wine style: LIVELY RED
GEORGES DUBOEUF 08 BEAUJOLAIS, FRANCE
212480 $12.05

wine style: LIVELY RED
BOUCHARD PÈRE & FILS 08 BEAUJOLAIS-VILLAGES, FRANCE 665448 $12.75

Li
LIVELY RED

THE LIGHTER SHADE OF PINOT

What I love about this style of Pinot Noir is how it invites us to celebrate light over dark. Lively over smooth. Playful over serious. In some cases, it can be as lighthearted as Beaujolais. Love that.

Wouldn't it be great if light red wine were to become as popular and as acceptable as light beers. Something for our local wine industry to get working on!

The Cave Spring Pinot is a beautiful expression of lightness and brightness. Could be related to Beaujolais. Could score in the top ten of great light reds. Create the scene and the wine will come through for you.

Inniskillin's Pinot is in a similar style. A shade lighter and leaner but a super-refresher for daytime sipping. Bocce, anyone?

BEST TIMES: *Drinking in the day. Lunch or light meals.*

wine style: LIVELY RED

CAVE SPRING CELLARS 07 PINOT NOIR, VQA NIAGARA

4176420$16.95

wine style: LIVELY RED

INNISKILLIN 07 PINOT NOIR 'VARIETAL SERIES', VQA NIAGARA

261099 $14.75

PICNIC PINOT

Italian producer Lamberti, has a delicate touch with their wines in the Santepietre line. The newly arrived Pinot could be the best light red in the stores. It has delicious fruitiness, a lively, vivacious personality – an awfully good, everyday drink. The Honda Civic of wines!

Wine geeks are sure to tell you that it doesn't have much Pinot character. To which you reply: "Frankly, I don't give a damn." There's always someone trying to spoil the fun. And Lamberti's wine is all about having fun. One of the best new wines of the year.

Most of the Two Oceans line of wines are a bit `commercially nice´ but I really like their Pinot because of its smokey quality. This is the Pinot if your picnic involves a grill. The combination of sweet berry fruit and smokiness could not be more prefect for partnering with BBQ'd foods – chicken, salmon, sausages, burgers, etc. Two Oceans could do wonders for your cooking! Not to mention your budget.

Li
LIVELY RED

BEST TIMES: *Picnics, lunch, afternoons, BBQs, light meals.*

wine style: LIVELY RED

LAMBERTI 07 PINOT NOIR 'SANTEPIETRE', VENEZIE, ITALY

74070 $11.95 UNDER $12

wine style: LIVELY RED

TWO OCEANS 08 PINOT NOIR, SOUTH AFRICA

61598 $9.95 UNDER $12

BRINGING BACK THE OLD RHÔNE RULE

Before Australia, and more recently Argentina, dominated the wine market there was a golden rule for novice drinkers: "You can't go wrong with a Côtes du Rhône." This wine was friendly, had great drinkability and was affordable. Every restaurant used to carry it and it matched well with white or red meat. I'd like to bring back this rule because the quality and value of Côtes du Rhône has never been better.

On this page you'll meet a few light Rhônes and there's more of the family in the Rustic and Rich Red sections. Light Rhônes are the everyday reds of this region – they're a bit like Beaujolais in their invitation to gulp. And they're also very food friendly.

The usually dull Rodet has come alive in the 08 vintage with a great blast of fruitiness and liveliness. Refreshing and fun. Hard to stop gulping this.

Mommessin keeps improving too. This Rhône is juicy, vibrant and awfully good. I like the feeling – somewhere between lighthearted and nourishing. Was Joni drinking this when she wrote "A Case of You" ?

BEST TIMES: *Côtes du Rhône and a roasted chicken always make me happy.*

FYI: Mommessin, Louis Bernard and Bouchard Aine & Fils have all improved since being taken over by the Boisset company. Boisset was one of the founders of Le Clos Jordanne in Niagara.

Li
LIVELY
RED

wine style: LIVELY RED

RODET 08 CÔTES DU RHÔNE, FRANCE
8979 $12.80

UNDER $12

wine style: LIVELY RED

MOMMESSIN 08 CÔTES DU RHÔNE 'LES EPICES', FRANCE 14829 $11.85

ITALY IS THE KING OF LIGHT RED

Observe the style of red wine poured and enjoyed at an Italian café – pale and light. For some of the customers it's an hourly thing. A glass of refreshment. Maybe if we did more daily tippling we'd be bigger fans of light reds. We'd appreciate lightness and liveliness.

Valpolicella is Italy's best know light red. It used to be everywhere and not very good, but now there's less of it and the quality has improved. The popularity of Ripasso and Amarone (rich editions of Valpolicella) has also improved the image.

Lamberti's wine is a good mix of traditional earthiness and modern bright flavours. Tangy and super-refreshing. A few gulps and you're in Italy. With a little antipasto, of course. Food always brings out the best in Italian wines.

Tommasi crafts Valpolicella in a juicy, vibrant, Beaujolais style. Delightful, charming and playful. A lovely early evening wine to sip as you prepare supper. I drink a lot of this. Too bad about the crass `88´ wine score stuck on the bottle.

BEST TIMES: *The mood to be at an Italian café.*

wine style: LIVELY RED UNDER $12

LAMBERTI 08 VALPOLICELLA 'SANTEPIETRE', VENETO, ITALY 560508 $11.25

wine style: LIVELY RED

TOMMASI 08 VALPOLICELLA, VENETO, ITALY
669150 $13.95

Ru

RUSTIC

GUTSY
SOLID & HEARTY
EARTHY
THE REAL DEAL
LOTS OF ENERGY
ITALIAN
INVIGORATING
A BIT CHALLENGING
COMPLEMENTARY
FOOD
PARTNER

RUSTIC REDS

TRUE TO THEIR ROOTS

Cabernet and Merlot originated in Bordeaux, France where they're still going strong. But everyday Bordeaux does not taste anything like the Aussie or Chilean versions of these grapes. A cool climate and French wine culture produces a light and lean red – Bistro style wine. Bordeaux is great with food, but not a lot of fun for party gulping especially if you have a low tolerance for dryness.

I enjoy Bordeaux in the summer and fall for their refreshing nature and moderate alcohol levels. Their rustic bite makes a change from more easy-going wines.

Medoc is a region in Bordeaux and Calvet's wine is gutsy and invigorating. Traditional French-style red that suggests elbows on the table and `let's-get-eating´. Bring on the second bottle.

wine style: RUSTIC RED

CALVET 06 MEDOC, BORDEAUX, FRANCE

38208 $13.95

I'm delighted to be able to include golden oldie Mouton Cadet this year. It's never tasted better. Expect the refreshing qualities of the Calvet along with a mannered, modest feeling. None of the look-at-me qualities of modern wines. Good dinner company, for sure.

BEST TIMES: *Traditional bistro foods – roasts, grills, casseroles. A night around the dinner table with no discussion of wine – just drinking it.*

wine style: RUSTIC RED

MOUTON CADET 07 BORDEAUX, FRANCE

943 $14.25

Ru
RUSTIC RED

A WALK IN THE CANADIAN WOODS

Our most 'Canadian' wine is Baco Noir. It captures the rustic, outback feeling of the Canadian landscape. Toss in wild, unrefined and big-hearted and you have the wine equivalent of Gordon Lightfoot songs or Tom Thomson paintings. Hardly any other place grows Baco, so it's an exclusive .

Henry of Pelham is the gatekeeper of Baco and the 07 Vintage is as gutsy and challenging as in previous years. Boldness and vigour over niceness and smoothness. Wine to partner with food.

Sandbanks from Prince Edward County has joined the Baco clan with a wine that has the rustic-meets-charming quality of Neil Young's voice.

BEST TIMES: *The bitter edge in Baco is great at stimulating the appetite, and keeping it so. Hearty, rustic food – burgers, sausages, etc.*

wine style: RUSTIC RED

HENRY OF PELHAM 07 BACO NOIR, VQA ONTARIO

270926 $13.65

wine style: RUSTIC RED

SANDBANKS ESTATE WINERY 07 BACO NOIR, VQA ONTARIO 110049 $14.95

DOING THE DROIT

The Droit clone produces a more substantial wine than the regular Gamays. An earthy character with gamey flavours. If you're up for a trip outside the ordinary this is a must try.

Château des Charmes' 07 is quite raunchy and farmyard-ish. Bordering on rich. Classic French country-style wine that makes no sense without food. Will appeal to those who enjoy adventure. One of the most interesting and overlooked local wines in the store.

BEST TIMES: *A few cheeses, a baguette, a checkered tablecloth and life will be good. Lightly chill the wine. Also a perfect partner for coq au vin or anything bistro-ish. The Julie & Julia movie wine.*

wine style: RUSTIC RED

CH. DES CHARMES 07 GAMAY 'DROIT', VQA ST. DAVIDS BENCH 582353 $16.75

Ru
RUSTIC RED

PINOT FROM THE ISLAND AND THE MAINLAND

Pinot Noir is one of the current hot reds but it has limitations. There's not a lot of it, and it's usually expensive. Pelee Island to the rescue.

Ontario is producing small quantities of wonderful world-class Pinots, but my favourite is this fifteen-dollar edition coming from Pelee Island. Whereas Pinot is usually pretty, this wine is more rustic. The earthy, tangy flavours remind me of traditional Italian wines. A great partner for a simple roasted chicken or tomato pasta. But you can expect this wine to become more seductive in a year's time.

Pelham is another producer of reasonably priced Pinot and their 07 also has some gutsy Italian character. Grabs the taste buds and demands some food on the table. There's an authentic feeling and a strong sense of the earth.

BEST TIMES: *Pinot is lighter than other reds so it goes with meats other than beef or lamb. Grilled salmon or wild mushroom risotto with Pinot is a no-brainer.*

wine style: RUSTIC RED

PELEE ISLAND 08 PINOT NOIR RESERVE, VQA PELEE ISLAND 135939 $14.75

wine style: RUSTIC RED

HENRY OF PELHAM 07 PINOT NOIR, VQA NIAGARA 13904 $17.10

THE ITALIAN TABLE

Italy is rustic. Millions of tourists visit to roam the hills and wonky villages where nothing has changed in a thousand years. Saturdays are spent at traditional markets and tavernas, not Home Depot.

Italian life has an edge and a vitality – in art, sport, food and family life – and in Italian wines too. Gusto and vigour are prized over smoothness. Live a little more Italian with the following reds.

Spinelli's Sangiovese is earthy, gutsy, tangy dry. A lot of refreshment at first, nourishing later – the Italian experience. Buy a case so you can have it every day.

You'll find a similar experience in Casal Thaulero Sangiovese. A touch fuller but there's lots of pucker to partner food. Think hearty.

FYI: Abruzzi is next door to Tuscany and Sangiovese is the grape of Chianti.

BEST TIMES: *Everyday foods and any old time. Wine, conversation and second helpings.*

wine style: RUSTIC RED

SPINELLI 08 SANGIOVESE, ABRUZZI, ITALY

UNDER $12

621961 $7.50

wine style: RUSTIC RED

CASAL THAULERO 08 SANGIOVESE, ABRUZZI, ITALY

UNDER $12

588996 $7.50

GIVE ME THE ORIGINAL STYLE CHIANTI

One of my disappointments with the modern wine world is the movement to please everyone. Original character is on the decline and an example of this is the Chianti wines.

Today, most of the Chiantis and other reds coming from Tuscany are crafted to please a worldwide audience. The traditional, gutsy, rustic character has been smoothed over with vanilla flavouring and other crowd-pleasing techniques.

But all is not lost. You can still get a hit of Chianti with Rocca delle Macie. A wild wine that feels like it never left Italy. Bring on the food and banish your cares.

Castiglioni also delivers the true Tuscan experience. Gutsy Chianti with a happy heart – part rustic, part rich. Pleases in an effortless way. I'd be happy to have this with most meals on most days.

BEST TIMES: *Doing the Italian thing – wine, food and friends.*

wine style: RUSTIC RED

ROCCA DELLE MACIE 08 CHIANTI 'VERNAIOLO', TUSCANY, ITALY

269589 $13.45

wine style: RUSTIC RED

FRESCOBALDI 07 CHIANTI 'CASTIGLIONI', TUSCANY, ITALY

545319 $14.65

RUSTIC BEAUJOLAIS

Most Beaujolais falls into my Lively Red category but some of the stuff wants to go a little deeper in feeling. I love both styles for their honesty and drinkability.

Rustic Beaujolais takes on some of the character of Pinot Noir – earthy, gamey – an invitation to the French bistro mood. Bistro restaurants favour this earthy style because it's a great food partner.

Bouchard's wine couldn't be more French – bring on the poulet. And a second bottle. Duboeuf's is a very gulpable, instant feel-good wine. More chicken, more wine please.

BEST TIMES: *Doing the Bistro thing.*

wine style: RUSTIC RED

BOUCHARD AÎNÉ & FILS 08 BEAUJOLAIS SUPÉRIEUR, FRANCE 9431 $12.45

Ru
RUSTIC RED

wine style: RUSTIC RED

GEORGES DUBOEUF 08 BEAUJOLAIS-VILLAGES, FRANCE 122077 $12.95

THE NEW PORTUGAL

You have to admire Portugal's stance in the wine world. When everyone else aligned with the popular grape varieties, Portugal took the gamble of sticking with its native grapes. It's now in the position of being able to offer an alternative to Cabernet, Merlot and Shiraz. Whether enough people want alternatives is the big unknown.

If you do, I'm happy to report that you'll be more than pleased with a lot of the current crop. The three reds opposite deserve to be as popular as Fuzion. Maybe more so.

Vila Regia is a good place to start Portuguese-*ing*. Delicious fruitiness combined with earthiness and a light feeling. Excellent house wine. Note the price.

For something more gutsy, try Flor de Crasto. Vitality and purity are the show here – Chianti-like. Refreshingly wild and real. We need more wines with this kind of spunk.

Alianca's Bairrada in the most hearty of the trio. Rustic and loaded with solid, earthy flavours. It's the backwoods, the pickup truck, the pot roast. Wine with a big heart, and a gentle price. It's been in almost every edition of this book.

BEST TIMES: *A mood for down-to-earth reds. Wines with the feeling of a place. For food – not party drinks.*

wine style: RUSTIC RED UNDER $12

SOGRAPE VINHOS 06 DOURO 'VILA REGIA', PORTUGAL 464388 $8.75

wine style: RUSTIC RED

QUINTA DO CRASTO 07 DOURO 'FLOR DE CRASTO', PORTUGAL 89870 $10.75

UNDER $12

Ru
RUSTIC RED

UNDER $12

wine style: RUSTIC RED

ALIANCA 06 BAIRRADA RESERVA, PORTUGAL

158741 $8.50

DAN SULLIVAN winemaker at Rosehall Run winery, Prince Edward County

Q: IS IT MY IMAGINATION, OR DO A LOT OF RED WINES TASTE THE SAME?

A: You're right, especially if you're drinking the popular brands. A few years ago, wineries noticed that all the big selling reds were rich, fruity, smooth and a little sweet. This style has now become the prototype for red wines from all over the world. Blame Australia for starting it but now others have copied them. One of the reasons I review wines is to offer alternative choices. The appeal of wine is its diversity and that's still there if you seek it out.

Q: CAN YOU PASS ALONG ONE TIP I CAN USE TONIGHT AT HOME?

A: Buy and OPEN three bottles. Have three experiences instead of just one. Have a glass of each, re-cork and refrigerate your stash – ready to repeat the following night…and for as many evenings as it takes to finish the bottles. You won't believe how much more FUN this is than the traditional `same wine all evening´. Plus the contrast from one wine to the next will open your eyes to the magic of experiencing the best wine for your mood. And you'll be conducting your very own wine school.

Q: WHICH CATEGORY OF WINE DO YOU BUY MOST OFTEN?

A: FRESH whites and RUSTIC reds. I start every evening with a glass or two of FRESH and move on to RUSTIC. RUSTIC is the wine category most suited to meals because it stimulates the palate and flatters food. RUSTIC is the tomato sauce of wines – it makes everything taste better. I usually drink RICH reds after dinner.

DON'T BE AFRAID OF TART

Everyday Burgundy has three strikes against it: it's pricy, pale in colour and tart. And it's the lightest edition of Pinot Noir in the world – so make that four strikes. But can I sell you a bottle?

Italy's Barbera is refreshing, food-friendly and affordable. But it's tart.

Let me explain the benefits of tartness, and why Europeans love it. Tartness refreshes, stimulates the appetite and lifts flavours out of food. It's your best friend when drinking and eating. Give tart a chance and it will reward you better than Air Miles.

Chose tart, lively reds in the summer or anytime you're in the mood for refreshment. Patriarche Pinot comes with a little Burgundy barnyard flavour and lots of bistro gusto. With a little imagination you might find yourself into a two bottle evening. Tartness does that.

Barbera is only produced in the Piedmont region of Italy where it's the everyday drink. The locals know. Most Barberas are now softened up for the export market, but thankfully we still have Bersano. The real deal. Full of vitality and earthy authenticity. Sort of pale in the style of Pinot and every bit as refreshing. I call it my good-with-food Beaujolais.

BEST TIMES: *Picnics or light suppers. Lightly chill.*

wine style: RUSTIC RED

PATRIARCHE 07 PINOT NOIR, BURGUNDY, FRANCE

23903 $16.25

wine style: RUSTIC RED

BERSANO 07 BARBERA D'ASTI 'COSTALUNGA', PIEDMONT, ITALY 348680 $12.95

A NIGHT AT THE BISTRO

There seems to be a bistro revival. Small neighbourhood restaurants are adopting the name as a way of letting customers know their food is affordable and the place is friendly. I've even seen a deli franchise attach the word bistro to its name.

Bistro no longer means just French food and wine, but it's a good time to revisit French wines as they are much improved and are now reasonably priced. Especially those from the south.

Ch. de Gourgazaud is a classic bistro red – country wildness meets nourishing. Traditional rustic wine character meets easy drinking. Think of it as Shiraz's younger cousin – drier tasting, more earthy and really good with food. Especially on fall or winter nights. Gourgazaud should be one of the LCBOs top-sellers.

La Vieille Ferme is a juicy, spirited red in the style of Côtes du Rhône. Feels playful as well as nourishing. The Toyota of reds – good and affordable. Everyday wine doesn't get much better.

BEST TIMES: *At the super table with grills, roasts, pastas. Don't be caught with just a single bottle.*

wine style: RUSTIC RED

CH. DE GOURGAZAUD 07 MINERVOIS, FRANCE

22384 $12.80

Ru
RUSTIC RED

wine style: RUSTIC RED

LA VIEILLE FERME 07 CÔTES DU VENTOUX, FRANCE

263640 $11.75 UNDER $12

THREE REALLY GOOD EVERYDAY REDS

We associate Merlot, Shiraz and Malbec with richness but it ain't always so. These grapes can be crafted in a rustic, refreshing style. Wines that don't kill you with high alcohol and which are ideal with everyday meals and times.

Cesari Merlot is a taste of everyday Italian life – lots of vitality, vibrant flavours and the all important invitation to eat. One sip and you want food. Tasted with food the wine feels special and starts to sing. You are living well – keep pouring.

The Yvon Mau wine is seriously rustic. I love the honest, country feeling, and the sense of a place. It also invites you to have food, and will support your appetite all night long. Johnny Cash might have enjoyed this – nourishment with a hard edge.

Trapiche wines are often commercially `nice´ but I like the vibrancy, refreshing bite and light touch here. Shades of Italy. If you enjoy gusto, add this to your house wine list. Sip while you prepare supper.

BEST TIMES: *An alternative to heavy reds.*

wine style: RUSTIC RED

CESARI 08 MERLOT, VENEZIE, ITALY 572453 $7.25 UNDER $12

UNDER $12

wine style: RUSTIC RED

YVON MAU 08 SHIRAZ, VDP DE L'AUDE, FRANCE

621979 $9.75

UNDER $12

wine style: RUSTIC RED

TRAPICHE 08 MALBEC, MENDOZA, ARGENTINA

501551 $8.95

ONTARIO DOES EUROPE

The role model for Ontario reds is the north of France and Italy – regions that also have a temperate climate and which produce wines with a pure, dry, refreshing character. And which are moderate in alcohol, flavour and richness. These characteristics make for good food partners because they stimulate the appetite. The last thing we should expect of local red wine is lots of richness and lushness.

Cabernet Franc is Ontario's bistro red. Spend an evening with Ch. des Charmes wine for an invigorating French country experience. Rustic and real. Coyote's Run Cabernet (50/50 Cab Sauv and Cab Franc) is a wonderfully pure expression of these grapes – gutsy, challenging, refreshing. A classic bistro-style red that says "Bring on the food and friends – and another bottle." We need more local reds in this style.

And here's another one, from Creekside – the masters of Niagara Shiraz. I call this my local Chianti because it has so much vitality. Feels richer than local Cabs because of the deep, earthy flavours but the vigorous side keeps it in the rustic camp.

Meritage is a word for the Bordeaux blend of Cabernet and Merlot and this style is usually big and hefty. However, Hillebrand offers a lighter, everyday edition – that they put in clear glass so you get the message of it being a lively, cheerful "Where's my pasta?" wine. With screw cap.

BEST TIMES: *At the supper table with friends and everyday foods.*

wine style: RUSTIC RED

CH. DES CHARMES 07 CABERNET FRANC, VQA NIAGARA-ON-THE-LAKE 277236 $13.95

wine style: RUSTIC RED

COYOTE'S RUN 07 CABERNET, VQA NIAGARA
26757 $16.30

wine style: RUSTIC RED

CREEKSIDE 07 SHIRAZ, VQA NIAGARA
66654 $15.75

wine style: RUSTIC RED

HILLEBRAND 07 MERITAGE 'ARTIST SERIES', VQA NIAGARA 56390 $13.05

RUSTIC AND ROMANTIC

Rioja was the original romantic red. If seduction was your plan, then Rioja was your wine.

The Rioja region developed the practice of ageing wines in American oak casks which imparts a sweetish, spicy, vanilla flavour. We are all suckers for vanilla and most regions now use oak of some form to enhance their wine's flavour and appeal. Some overdo it, and sales go through the roof. Rampant seduction.

Campo Viejo is an excellent bistro edition of Rioja. Rustic, invigorating and crying out for food. Not obviously seductive at first but guaranteed to add romance and an exotic feeling to a special, or a simple, supper. The power of wine to improve your mood.

Campo Viejo is an international brand that can be a lifesavor in situations where everything in the store is foreign or suspect. Enter it in your iPhone or Blackberry.

BEST TIMES: *A little romance.*

wine style: RUSTIC RED

CAMPO VIEJO 06 RIOJA CRIANZA, SPAIN

620997$14.45

NOTES

Ri

RICH

MELLOW
SEDUCTIVE
ROMANTIC
SUBSTANTIAL
POWERFUL
CHILLING OUT
SLOW
CONTEMPLATIVE
IMPRESSIVE
LOW ENERGY

RICH REDS

BABY RICH

Pinot Noir is hard to pin down. It looks pale, feels light but after a glass or two it changes the game. You notice richness – and the wine feels bigger and in some cases, very sexy.

Fans of Pinot know about this, but I wanted the rest of you to understand the seduction process.

Prospect's Pinot has a laid-back California feeling. Spicy/sweet and showing off. A wine style that's great with Tex/Mex foods. Funnily enough it becomes more lively with food – really brightens up. Fun stuff.

Wine geeks would describe Inniskillin's wine as a `nice little Pinot´. And they'd be almost right. While there are only moderate amounts of flavour and richness, there's no shortage of charm and vitality. Playful, very gulpable in the bistro style. Inniskillin pioneered Pinot in Niagara and while others have taken it to greater heights they still deliver in the more affordable price range.

Mondavi is the George Clooney of Pinot – a mega charmer. Playing all the tricks in the book and doing it well. Could be the most seductive red in the stores. Not a lot of flesh on the bone so choose bird over beef. Try Pinot and herbed chicken – the classic sexy meal.

BEST TIMES: *Looking for charm.*

Ontario wineries making premium Pinot Noir:
LAILEY, FLAT ROCK, MALIVOIRE, TAWSE LE CLOS JORDANNE, NORMAN HARDIE, ROSEHALL RUN, LONG DOG, KEINT-HE and CLOSSON CHASE.

wine style: RICH RED

PROSPECT WINERY 07 PINOT NOIR 'FATS JOHNSON', VQA OKANAGAN 92304 $15.95

wine style: RICH RED

INNISKILLIN 08 PINOT NOIR 'RESERVE', VQA NIAGARA 669390 $18.25

Ri
RICH RED

wine style: RICH RED

ROBERT MONDAVI 07 PINOT NOIR 'PRIVATE SELECTION', CALIFORNIA 465425 $18.95

ARRIVE IN STYLE

The LCBO has copied lots of my ideas so why shouldn't I borrow one of their slogans! Sometimes you need, or want, a wine that looks like it has class. No critters or flowers on the label – just the traditional black and white look. And the classic Bordeaux blend of Cabernet and Merlot.

It also helps if the wine lives up to appearances. Lots of character, but not too serious. My three offerings deliver good looks and a friendly personality.

Hillebrand's Trius Red was created by the French man, J.L. Groux, (now at Stratus) and the tall elegant bottle always gets a wow. Fun to pour too. The 07 vintage is richer than usual – lots of impact with New World drinkability. Sure to impress.

Bordeaux is all about tradition and ritzy prices but a few owners are delivering the experience in the twenty-dollar range. Ch. Pey la Tour hits the middle ground between the reserved character of Bordeaux and good drinkability. Lovely grace and charm. Just give it time to open up to you, and vice versa.

The Malbec grape originated in Bordeaux, but now it's Argentina's hot new wine. Catena's Malbec combines the very dry Bordeaux nature with the rich, ripe flavours of South American reds. Classy wine that's fun to drink. You're bound to get complements.

BEST TIMES: *Dinner parties with traditional grilled/roasted lamb or beef.*

wine style: RICH RED

HILLEBRAND 07 TRIUS RED, VQA NIAGARA

303800 VE $21.95

wine style: RICH RED

CH. PEY LA TOUR 06 BORDEAUX, FRANCE

925859 VE $22.95

wine style: RICH RED

CATENA 07 MALBEC, MENDOZA, ARGENTINA

478727 VE $19.95

Ri
RICH RED

VE* Vintages Essentials - always available

CHIANTI: THE HEARTBEAT OF ITALY

Chianti is the Holy Grail of Italian red wine. It delivers the contradictions in the Italian spirit – challenging meets loving. And the dichotomy of the rustic-meets-elegant found in the Italian landscape. Unless you know Italy you might not understand Chianti, or enjoy drinking it.

Unfortunately much of the Chianti wine industry has sold its soul to the international, crowd-pleasing wine style (smooth) and there isn't much of the real thing available anymore. But I did find a few traditionalists – individuals in a wine world overrun with sameness.

Rocca delle Macie's wine is classic Chianti, feeling both rustic and rich. It suggests the Tuscan country-side – the earth, the history, the simplicity and the elegance. Impressive, without pretence.

The Brolio estate is credited with creating the first Chianti. The story goes that the Count couldn't find a girlfriend so he devoted himself to vineyards instead! A bit like how the monks developed Burgundy. Brolio delivers the gutsy Chianti experience with richness and a romantic feeling. Steakhouse Chianti.

BEST TIMES: *A mood for a semi-rich red with a sense of place and history.*

wine style: RICH RED

ROCCA DELLE MACIE 07 CHIANTI CLASSICO, TUSCANY, ITALY 741769 VE $18.95

wine style: RICH RED

RICASOLI 07 CHIANTI 'BROLIO', TUSCANY, ITALY

3962 $23.95

VE* Vintages Essentials

STEPPING UP TO THE PLATE

Here's two local reds that are nudging into the league of Rich Reds.

For a delish Merlot that's not too gushy or plummy, check out Innikskillin. I'm not usually a fan of soft and smooth, but it feels good here. Comforts without smothering. Could be the yummiest $15 local red. Equally good with red or white meats.

Pelee's wine is only semi-rich but scores for charm and mellow sweetness. Sure to be well-received at family and holiday events. A Cab/Merlot blend with the feeling of the latter. It's interesting to see Pelee break out of the flora and bird theme with this new line of wines that are helping support Ontario food banks.

BEST TIMES: *Looking for locally made comfort reds.*

wine style: RICH RED

INNISKILLIN 07 MERLOT 'VARIETAL SERIES', VQA ONTARIO 323444 $15.45

wine style: RICH RED

PELEE ISLAND 08 CAB/MERLOT 'STEPPING UP TO THE PLATE', VQA ONTARIO 435321 $12.75

IF YOU WANT CHARM START DATING GRENACHE

Grenache is the undercover guy responsible for a lot of the most charming reds in the world. For some reason he shies away from publicity and his name seldom appears in the credits. So the price is usually low.

Grenache's playground is the South of France and North of Spain. Good places to play. It forms the backbone for most of the dry Rosés of France and Spain. And it's the reason Côtes du Rhône is one of the most delicious everyday reds on the planet.

The 07 Sangre de Toro is a five star charmer. Bright, modern wine in a dark, traditional package. Grenache (called Garnacha in Spain) is the poor man's Pinot. Get a bottle and you'll see what I mean.

The new vintage of Goats has killer charm. Bright, spicy flavours and a lively personality – so fun to drink. Sensational value too. Goats do Roam is a play on Côtes du Rhône. Even though it isn't made with Grenache it captures that grapes's charming spirit.

BEST TIMES: *The mood for a budget-priced charming red.*

UNDER $12

wine style: RICH RED

TORRES 07 SANGRE DE TORO, CATALONIA, SPAIN

6585 $11.75

wine style: RICH RED

CHARLES BECK 07 'GOATS DO ROAM' RED, SOUTH AFRICA

718940 VE $12.95

VE* Vintages Essentials

MERRY MERLOT

Merlot gets flack for being too popular. For sure some of the stuff is boringly nice, but don't write off the entire clan. California in particular delivers Merlot with lots of charm and vitality.

I discovered Maxie's at a party. The hostess said it was her house red. "Works well all the time." It certainly worked for me that night so I bought a bottle to see if it was just my party mood. But no, Maxie's Dog House is damn good house wine. Rich, with a playful feeling. The hostess was right.

Carmen Merlot is a great bottle of fun for the price. Juicy and appetizing. Wonderful vibrancy. No commercial niceness here, this is darn good stuff. Could be all you need. (Check out Carmen Cabernet too).

There's traditional wine character – a sense of the

wine style: RICH RED
DOG HOUSE 06 'MAXIE'S MERLOT', CALIFORNIA
614156 $13.75

wine style: RICH RED
CARMEN 08 MERLOT, CHILE
248625 $10.70
UNDER $12

earth, in Mondavi's wine. And it's developing nourishing, woodsy, fall day feelings. Just a great show. A nice decanter and a little imagination will take this experience to the top level. Serve with beef or lamb.

Beringer Merlot is also awfully good. A great mix of Old World solidness and gorgeous New World flavours. Classy meets flashy. Delivers premium quality with charm.

BEST TIMES: *Dare to do Merlot.*

wine style: RICH RED

ROBERT MONDAVI 06 MERLOT 'PRIVATE SELECTION', CALIFORNIA

524769 $18.95

wine style: RICH RED

BERINGER 06 MERLOT 'FOUNDER'S ESTATE', CALIFORNIA

534255 $19.95

RED FRINGE FESTIVAL

These are my Tom Waits wines. Soulful, independent spirits, hoping to find an audience. Wines outside the Cab/Merlot/Shiraz (and now Malbec) family have difficulty getting airplay. Please support diversity and check out the following. Who knows, you may stay on the fringe side.

Roodeberg has survived decades of wine trends and I feel it may well go on forever. This is the 60th vintage! Earthy, gutsy stuff with a back-woods, cottage feeling. And the whiff-of-smoke character of many South African reds. Mildly rich and an all season performer – summer BBQs, hearty foods in winter.

If you live in a solid red brick house, you may indentify with the solid nature of Vista TN. Feels like a blend of every red in the world. Confident, earthy wine for roast beef. Touriga Nacional is the principal grape of Port.

Terra d'Aligi is a hefty edition of the seven-dollar Spinelli red in the Rustic section. Dark, dense and very beefsteak-ish. Fringe wine with an old-fashioned, warm-hearted feeling.

The blockbuster in this group is Almasa from Spain. The super-concentrated, spicy/sweet flavours may remind you of your favourite Shiraz. Yummy barely describes the experience. Bargain of a lifetime if you're into excess.

Carmenere has the plummy richness of Merlot along with smokey, peppery flavours. Some find it odd, but I like the something different quality. Worth a detour.

BEST TIMES: *Taking a break from the same old.*

wine style: RICH RED

KWV 07 ROODEBERG, SOUTH AFRICA 7187 $12.55

wine style: RICH RED

CAVES ALIANCA 06 'VISTA TN', TOURIGA NACIONAL, BEIRAS, PORTUGAL 613919 $13.00

wine style: RICH RED

SPINELLI 06 'TERRA D'ALIGI', MONTEPULCIANO D'ABRUZZO, ITALY 28530 $11.95

UNDER $12

wine style: RICH RED

BODEGAS PIQUERAS 05 CASTILLO DE ALMANSA RESERVA, SPAIN 270363 $11.85

UNDER $12

Ri
RICH RED

wine style: RICH RED

CONCHA Y TORO 08 CARMENERE 'CASILLERO DEL DIABLO', CHILE

620666 $12.95

RICH ON A BUDGET

There was a time when you had to pay a lot of money for a really rich red wine. Only the rich drank rich. But not anymore. Today we're swimming in richness at mall prices.

This gang are on the high end of rich. Not for ladies lunches, or even power lunches. But who am I to say what to drink with lunch!

Railroad red is aptly named. A manly, heavy metal experience. Or a bit like sitting front row at the Calgary Stampede. Go for the gusto guys! But is quite a lively wine for something so rich.

There are lots of Abruzzi wines in this book with Casale Vecchio being the big daddy. Lush, rich and warmhearted. Not my style but millions will love it.

Also weighing in at half a ton is Perez Cruz. The show of flavours is amazing – plummy, spicy,

wine style: RICH RED

GRAHAM BECK 07 SHIRAZ/ CABERNET 'RAILROAD RED', SOUTH AFRICA 665273 $12.20

wine style: RICH RED

FARNESE 07 MONTEPULCIANO D'ABRUZZO, 'CASALE VECCHIO', ITALY 612788 $12.10

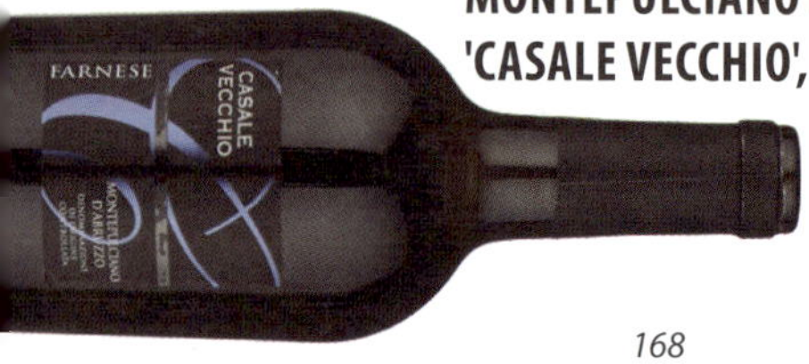

leathery, smokey – something for everyone. Ready for battle with any large hunk of meat slathered in sauce.

Rhône reds usually have a woodsy, fall day-in-the-country feeling, but La Romaine is more suggestive of a winter fireside. Deep, hefty flavours create a warming, nourishing feeling.

BEST TIMES: *Steak night.*

wine style: RICH RED

PEREZ CRUZ 07 CABERNET SAUVIGNON RESERVA, CHILE 694208 VE $14.75

wine style: RICH RED

CAVE LA ROMAINE 07 CÔTES DU RHÔNE-VILLAGE, FRANCE 28779 $12.75

Ri
RICH RED

VE* Vintages Essentials

THE RIPASSO BOYS

Ripasso is an enriched wine. The modest Valpolicella is given a little heft, so it can compete on the world stage. When well-crafted, Ripasso can be a wonderful combo of Italian vitality and richness. A middle ground wine that works really well with lots of foods.

The 06 Campofiorin of Masi is one of their best ever. Deep earthy flavours combined with an assured, confident feeling. The sense of something that's been around forever. Invites you to linger and spend the night. Best with primo meats, simply grilled. If possible, decant an hour before.

Cesari's wine is richer with Port-like flavours. Suggests a late evening hearty supper, or fireside sipping with cheese. And no cares.

BEST TIMES: *For hearty food.*

wine style: RICH RED
MASI 06 VALPOLICELLA RIPASSO 'CAMPOFIORIN', VENETO, ITALY 155051 $17.45

wine style: RICH RED
CESARI 06 VALPOLICELLA RIPASSO 'MARA', VENETO, ITALY
506519 $16.90

LET'S PLAY – ACT ONE

These wines remind me of the early days of pop music. Lots of love, lots of energy – a sweet innocence. Obvious niceness that somehow works.

Everyday Pinot and Zin are playful, joyful reds. Want to stay young? Have a bottle. It's a lot cheaper than going to your shrink.

Cono Sur comes with hit of spicy sweetness and refreshment. A playful lover. A lot of fun for the price. One glass leads to another, and another. And more fun.

Great drinkability and value are also strengths at Fetzer. Spicy sweetness and vitality too. Shades of Beaujolais that's been to modeling school – well made up and skilled in seduction. Be warned!

BEST TIMES: *Parties and private affairs. Both wines are really good with white meats or grilled salmon.*

UNDER $12

wine style: RICH RED

CONO SUR 08 PINOT NOIR, CHILE 361602 $10.95

wine style: RICH RED

FETZER 07 ZINFANDEL 'VALLEY OAKS', CALIFORNIA

234617 $14.95

Ri
RICH RED

Q: MY PARTNER LOVES RICH REDS BUT I LIKE LIGHTER ONES. ANY SUGGESTIONS?

A: I suggest having your style to start the meal and the RICH red a little later. Your partner's RICH red will taste even richer after the experience of a lighter wine, and you may start to enjoy a small amount of the RICH style in a late evening situation. Super-RICH reds are not great food partners – they're stars that don't like to share the stage. Having them later means they have their own space and you can fully savour the experience.

Q: WHAT'S MEANT BY OAKY WINES?

A: Oak imparts a sweet vanilla taste which just happens to be the most appealing flavour on the planet. The more something smells and tastes of vanilla, the more it sells. Almost all of today's best selling wines are flavoured with vanilla. Honest. This can be done by putting the wine into an oak barrel, or adding oak chips, or plain old flavouring. Vanilla also helps mask faults in wine or makes plain wines more appealing. Traditional European wines tend to be more natural (only mildly-flavoured or not at all) and taste less sweet. Non-flavoured wines are better for stimulating the appetite and letting the food shine. Be aware of your fondness, or not, for vanilla.

LET'S PLAY – ACT TWO

Time to meet more Pinot and Zin, and a playful Aussie. How do these players differ from Act One? Adults only! Could be scenes of you know what.

You'll also notice the prices have gone up. For which you get an HD wine – more intensity and more seduction. We're talking hot and heavy. Send the kids to bed.

Ravenswood is one of the kings of Zin and the 07 could not be more lush. I think they airbrush it! The flavours are spicy, sexy, gorgeous and what makes it all so appealing is the lively, playful spirit. Could not be more charming.

You'll find the luxury lounge feeling in Stoneleigh Pinot. Lots of swevet charm. However, this doll is starting to show a wrinkle or two giving her a

wine style: RICH RED

RAVENSWOOD 07 ZINFANDEL 'VINTNERS BLEND', CALIFORNIA

359257 VE $17.95

wine style: RICH RED

STONELEIGH 07 PINOT NOIR, MARLBOROUGH, NEW ZEALAND

54353 $19.75

characterful mature feeling. The Mrs. Robinson of Pinot.

Le Clos Jordanne is also developing a mature side. Pretty fruit flavours evolving into something gamey and sensual. Light the candles and bring on supper. Wine for those who don't mind a little splurge to create a romantic French feeling. With an outstanding Niagara wine.

Wakefield's wine is very Zinfandel-ish – tons of spicy, sweet flavours along with a warm cuddly feeling. Christmas Day by the fireside. Good cheer all round. The `promised land´, for sure.

wine style: RICH RED

LE CLOS JORDANNE 06 PINOT NOIR, 'VILLAGE RESERVE', VQA NIAGARA

Wine Rack Stores $25

wine style: RICH RED

WAKEFIELD 07 SHIRAZ/ CABERNET 'PROMISED LAND', AUSTRALIA

625343 $15.30

ITALY DOES MODERN

Traditionally Italian wines were labeled by region but there's a movement to start using grape names, especially the well known ones. And when the production is aimed at the expert market. Are you ready to try some Merlot, Cabernet and Syrah – Italian style?

The Abruzzi province is the `outlet store´ for Italian red wines. Rock bottom prices for good quality, traditional wines. Casal Thaulero's wine delivers Merlot plumminess, Cabernet solidness and a rustic Italian feeling – the Italian way. For hearty foods and folks. Why pay more?

Arancio's Syrah strikes a perfect balance between traditional and modern expression. It would work for either camp. Solid, house wine feeling. A bit reserved at first, but the Italian spirit comes out with food.

BEST TIMES: *Fall or winter house wines.*

wine style: RICH RED

CASAL THAULERO 08 MERLOT/CABERNET, ABRUZZO, ITALY 621953 $6.95

UNDER $12

wine style: RICH RED

ARANCIO 07 SYRAH, SICILY 621730 $12.75

UNDER $12

YOU NEED TO KNOW NEDERBURG

Why? Because this winery is making some of the best ten-dollar wines in the world. And now that they've jazzed up the package, they look good too. The Shiraz and Cab are quite different in style, but I want you to try both as an introduction to the amazing quality of Nederburg wines. Also check out the white in my Nice & Easy section.

The Shiraz is lively and lovely. A real charmer. A gulper. Not the blockbuster style – expect instead some of the delicate qualities of Pinot. A fab multi-purpose red.

Nederburg Cabernet has found a sweet spot between the dusty dryness of Bordeaux and the more fruity style of the New World. Earthy meets friendly. A trace of smokiness adds to the wine's BBQ appeal.

BEST TIMES: *For a Nederburg night. Or World Cup games.*

wine style: RICH RED UNDER $12

NEDERBURG 07 SHIRAZ 'THE WINEMASTER'S RESERVE', SOUTH AFRICA 527457 $10.95

wine style: RICH RED

NEDERBURG 07 CABERNET SAUVIGNON 'THE WINEMASTER'S RESERVE', SOUTH AFRICA

111526 $10.95

UNDER $12

FULL OF GRACE: THE VENETO SPIRIT

All the old wine regions of Europe have a recognizable feeling or spirit in their wines. This feeling is not due to a plan or tradition, it just happens when things are left to happen – over a long period. A wine DNA evolves. New World wine regions don't have this because they can't sit around for hundreds of years waiting for a spirit to develop. Are you crazy?

The spirit of Italy's Veneto region (around Verona, around lake Garda) is gentleness and grace. As found in the Valpolicella, Bardolino and Soave family of wines. They all have a good-buddy friendliness.

The Masi winery is a great ambassador for the Veneto spirit as you'll find in the following wines, one of which is actually from Tuscany. Bear with me.

I've always loved the pure expression in good Valpolicella and you'll find this in Serego Alighieri Rosso. It glows in the glass with a natural fruitiness, vitality and charm. Ageing in cherry wood barrels adds a touch of spicy sexiness. Vitality, charm and gentle too. Can I text you?? The winery is operated by Masi but owned by a descendant of Dante, so why shouldn't the wine be interesting?

Here's where you have to give me some license. The Bello Ovile wine is from Tuscany, but it has the gentle feeling of the Veneto because it was created by Masi. It's just starting to develop a lovely, mellow, elegant character. Light some candles.

BEST TIMES: *A traditional Italian dinner – veal perhaps.*

wine style: RICH RED

SEREGO ALIGHIERI 07 ROSSO DEL VERONESE, VENETO, ITALY 447326 $15.75

wine style: RICH RED

SEREGO ALIGHIERI-MASI 05 'PODERI DEL BELLO OVILE', TUSCANY, ITALY 73106 $17.95

Ri
RICH RED

PORTUGAL AT A CROSSROAD

Do you cater to modern taste or do you stay with tradition? This is the big question facing wineries of the Old World. Modern style, soft, slightly sweet wines outsell the drier, more challenging, traditional style wines. By far. And nearly all the people who rank wine by scores favour the sweetish, modern style.

I believe you can be successful crafting wines that express the best of both styles. Reducing the challenging side but still keeping the character. The following pair express the huge difference between the old and modern styles.

THE TRADITIONAL
Duque de Viseu is very traditional. Hearty and rustic. Would not go over well at a party, but from a large glass with a roast, by candlelight, it can be the dinner guest you have always wanted. The deep, earthy flavours come alive and nourish your belly and soul – the food tempers the wine's bite. Check it out.

THE MODERN
The formula for Crasto is simpler. Just open and be seduced. It's rich and slightly sweet – the wine style that is very popular today because it delivers instant gratification. There's a lot of oomph, which for many is the measurement of good wine. Spicy/sweet sauced foods are the go to go with this.

BEST TIMES: *Exploring the old and the new.*

wine style: RICH RED

SOGRAPE VINHOS 06 DAO 'DUQUE DE VISEU', PORTUGAL 546309 VE $13.95

wine style: RICH RED

QUINTA DO CRASTO 07 DOURO, PORTUGAL 81588 VE $14.95

Ri
RICH
RED

VE* Vintages Essentials – always available

OLD AUSSIE GUYS FOR WINTER DINNERS

The Aussie wine world is mainly about young reds with sweet, jammy flavours. Open a bottle, strike up the barbee and let's party. But where do the more serious Aussie reds fit in?

The first thing that happens to red wines after a few years of ageing is they become drier. They feel like they are in a suit as opposed to casual wear and they invite you to dinner instead of the party.

Peter Lehmann's `Clancy's´ has turned the corner from fruity to earthy. There's the array of flavours that surface in mature wines – some exotic, some bitter. All great with food. Put wine in decanter, grill steak or lamb chops and experience another side of Aussie reds.

Jacob's Creek is deep, dark and mysterious. Manly in the Bordeaux style. Oak paneling and leather chairs. Maybe some tweed. Needs a traditional roast.

BEST TIMES: *The winter season – fireside dining would be perfect.*

wine style: RICH RED

PETER LEHMANN 05 SHIRAZ/CABERNET/MERLOT 'CLANCY'S', BAROSSA, AUSTRALIA 611467 $18.80

wine style: RICH RED

JACOB'S CREEK 06 CABERNET SAUVIGNON RESERVE, AUSTRALIA

91751 $16.95

THE KING OF CABS

A few decades ago there was a tasting held in Paris to select the world's best Cabernet. At that time, California was starting to make claims that their wine was better than Bordeaux – the home of Cabernet. When the results were tabulated, the wine world went into shock. Both California and Bordeaux were losers – the winning wine was from Spain. A single vineyard Cabernet produced by Torres and called Mas la Plana.

Mas la Plana is neither available nor in the price range of this book, but Torres produces a more affordable Cabernet called Gran Coronas that's also capable of surprising with its quality. The 05 vintage is as dazzling as a Broadway musical – lots of richness, plushness and seductive spicy/sweet flavours. An irresistible combo of power and charm.

BEST TIMES: *Hearty dinners.*

wine style: RICH RED

TORRES 05 CABERNET SAUVIGNON RESERVA 'GRAN CORONAS', PENEDES, SPAIN 36483 VE $18.95

HEAVY HITTING CABS

Steaks are on the grill, guests are knocking back cocktails, and it's time to open some big reds. There's lots to choose from in this book, but if the night has an indulgent vibe, then a hefty Cab is sure to please and impress.

California is usually a good at impressing and the warm-hearted, spicy rich J. Lohr lets it all hang out. The hedonistic side of the wine is tempered with a refreshing bite – just enough to keep your appetite humming.

The Wolfman needs no introduction and his darker labels have the classy look for dinner parties. The Premium Selection is rock solid, a brick wall Cab that says pay attention. Fortunately there's a lush, charming side too. Strength and seduction. You get it all.

If you think Chile only does cheap and cheerful you need an evening with the Marques. This is a super-

wine style: RICH RED

J. LOHR 07 CABERNET SAUVIGNON 'SEVEN OAKS', PASO ROBLES, CALIFORNIA 656561 VE $20.95

concentrated wine – sit back and savour the wealth. The warm, toasty feeling of being by the fire at your country mansion. A little spicy sweetness adds to the seduction. Could seriously embarrass a lot of wines at twice, or five times, the price.

BEST TIMES: *Knock 'em dead dinner parties.*

wine style: RICH RED

WOLF BLASS 06 CABERNET SAUVIGNON 'PREMIUM SELECTION', AUSTRALIA

321927 VE $24.95

wine style: RICH RED

CONCHA Y TORO 06 CABERNET SAUVIGNON 'MARQUES DE CASA CONCHA', CHILE

337238 VE $19.95

VE* Vintages Essentials – always available

MEET YOUR MALBEC

Malbec is the hot new red from Argentina but how does it differ from Cabernet of Shiraz? Or does it?

Malbec was part of the original Bordeaux Cabernet Merlot blend so expect it to be similar to those guys. Especially the Merlot. The style varies from winery to winery but if you like rich, dark reds, Malbec will fit comfortably into your life. The everyday priced wines tend to be slightly sweet and the premium ones are drier and more serious.

Flichman's 'Misterio' is hugely popular due to its spicy/sweet nature. To quote the famous American wine critic, it has `globs of everything´.

Fuzion is a Shiraz/Malbec blend that has broken all sales records because it's easy drinking, and easy on the pocket. In its defence, I must say that it has

UNDER $12

wine style: RICH RED

FINCA FLICHMAN 08 MALBEC 'MISTERIO', MENDOZA, ARGENTINA

28803 $7.80

more traditional wine character than most best sellers. A little sweet, but also solid and earthy. Should develop nicely over the year.

I like the frank, non-commercial quality of Concha y Toro Malbec. A good mix of yummy flavours and earthy, French wine character. Not a bad combo. Modern bistro wine – for traditional grills or spicy/sweet sauced BBQs.

BEST TIMES: *With red meats.*

wine style: RICH RED UNDER $12

FAMILIA ZUCCARDI 09 SHIRAZ/MALBEC 'FUZION', MENDOZA, ARGENTINA 83188 $7.45

wine style: RICH RED

CONCHA Y TORO 08 MALBEC 'CASILLERO DEL DIABLO', CHILE 94060 $12.95

Ri
RICH RED

A FEW TAKES ON SHIRAZ

France is home, Australia made it popular, and now almost every country is doing Shiraz. And why not? It seems to adapt well to new places. The rich and spicy flavours are a constant, but the level of intensity and sweet impression varies from region to region, and winemaker to winemaker.

Wyndham claims to have made the first Shiraz in Australia and the wine is certainly textbook Aussie. Jammy sweet with a sexy lushness and richness. Go get it.

Nugan's Cookoothama delivers the Aussie style – lots of ripe, juicy flavour. But without excess. Friendly, chummy wine for the BBQ or the party.

Fish Hoek is a new Shiraz from South Africa that's dangerously gulpable. Delicious fruitiness and charm. Adult Beaujolais. A great new addition to the South African section.

Bellingham Shiraz is more substantial with deep flavours and a little smokiness. There's also has a refreshing tang and also an earthy quality that balances the richness. Beefy BBQ wine for sure.

For value and food-friendliness you cannot beat Concha y Toro from Chile. Rich but with the down-to-earth feeling of a bistro wine. Likes food better than parties. Wish there were more Shiraz crafted in this dry, appetizing style.

BEST TIMES: *The BBQ.*

wine style: RICH RED

WYNDHAM ESTATES 07 SHIRAZ 'BIN 555', AUSTRALIA 189416 $16.25

wine style: RICH RED

NUGAN ESTATE 07 SHIRAZ 'COOKOOTHAMA', AUSTRALIA 619460 $14.00

wine style: RICH RED

FISH HOEK 07 SHIRAZ, SOUTH AFRICA
143743 $9.95

wine style: RICH RED

BELLINGHAM 06 SHIRAZ, SOUTH AFRICA
554360 $13.65

wine style: RICH RED

CONCHA Y TORO 08 SHIRAZ 'CASILLERO DEL DIABLO', CHILE 568055 $12.95

GOOD VALUE CAB

Cabernet is Mr. Reliable in the red wine world. He's like the family restaurant where the menu is predictable. You know there will be enough food on your plate – no surprises. Cabernet grows best in hot weather so the best buys are usually from New World countries.

Caliterra's Cabernet is amazing. You couldn't get better for the price. So much flavour, vitality and good cheer. Easy to make friends with this guy.

Stepping up in heft and maybe more weekend-ish, is the always reliable Santa Rita Reserva. Manly, gutsy stuff for hearty meals.

Nugan's Cookoothama has lots of flavour and spirit. I call it my Aussie bistro red because of the gusto and how it calls out for food.

***BEST TIMES:** When you want straightforward nourishment. No frills.*

UNDER $12

wine style: RICH RED

CALITERRA 08 CABERNET SAUVIGNON RESERVA, CHILE 257329 $8.95

wine style: RICH RED

SANTA RITA 07 CABERNET SAUVIGNON RESERVA, CHILE

253872 $13.95

wine style: RICH RED

NUGAN ESTATE 07 CABERNET/MERLOT 'COOKOOTHAMA', AUSTRALIA

91660 $13.95

NOTES

Q: WINE IS GOOD FOR YOU! DRINK IN MODERATION! WHICH IS IT?

A: Wine is good for us because it slows us down, relieves stress and makes us feel good at the end of the day. I believe it works best when you do it all the time. Be Moderate but Every Day – don't be a weekend binger.

Q: DO YOU JUST RECOMMEND WHAT YOU LIKE?

A: That would make life easy. No, I believe that all categories of wine are valid and I look for good examples in all styles. I encourage people to have lots of `likes´ as it makes life more interesting.

FEEL THE POWER

Sometimes the occasion demands a wine exuding power and confidence. And you want to look like you can play with the big boys.

Premium priced Aussie and Chilean Shiraz have a seriousness and solidness that goes over well at steak dinners. And any situation with guys (and girls) in suits.

Penfolds is the most famous name in Aussie reds and they produce several wines in the $100+ category. The Thomas Hyland brand gets you close to the action for a lot less. Broad shouldered, manly and assertive. Serious wine for sure. But elegant too, of course. It will be noticed.

The Barossa Valley produces hefty, dense high-alcohol wines. Real men stuff. The king of this region is Peter Lehmann and his Shiraz is all about power – in flavour and in feeling. Slightly bitter and challenging at first but once you get over the shock there's a wonderful show of earthy flavours.

Max Reserva from Chile is super-rich and solid. Shiraz crafted in a dry, serious, masculine style. Very together, very powerful and sure to impress. Demands slow sipping. Should age well, and even find charm.

BEST TIMES: *Practicing being the new CEO.*

wine style: RICH RED

PENFOLDS 06 SHIRAZ 'THOMAS HYLAND', AUSTRALIA 611210 VE $19.95

wine style: RICH RED

PETER LEHMANN 06 SHIRAZ, BAROSSA VALLEY, AUSTRALIA 572875 $19.80

wine style: RICH RED

ERRAZURIZ 07 SHIRAZ 'MAX RESERVA', CHILE

614750 $17.65

HEY YOU! STOP IGNORING THE RHÔNE GUYS

One thing that really puzzles me is why more people don't buy Rhône reds. Côtes du Rhônes are every bit as yummy as all the popular reds and in many cases, they are better value. They also have a soulful presence and a sense of place – qualities missing in a lot of the popular, fruity flavoured brands.

Côtes du Rhônes are produced from a blend of Syrah (Shiraz) and Grenache grapes – one of the happiest marriages in wine (see my Grenache page). When the word Villages is added, it usually implies a richer wine.

Louis Bernard's wine goes right to your nourishment chakra. Warming and cuddly, with wonderful deep, earthy flavours. A lot of richness for the price. Handy screw cap.

Perrin's wine strikes a balance between richness and an everyday, bistro feeling. It has the Côtes du Rhône trademarks: peppery flavours, vigour and nourishment and a soulful quality. Very people, and food, friendly.

Rasteau is one of the top wine villages in the Rhône and Chapoutier's wine has generous flavours and richness. But still manages to feel lively and graceful. Very bistro in feeling, suggesting good times. A top LCBO performer for over a decade.

BEST TIMES: *Any home cooked meal.*

wine style: RICH RED
LOUIS BERNARD 07 CÔTES DU RHÔNE-VILLAGES, FRANCE 391458 $12.85

Ri RICH RED

wine style: RICH RED
PERRIN 07 RESERVE CÔTES DU RHÔNE, FRANCE 363457 VE $14.75

wine style: RICH RED
CHAPOUTIER 06 RASTEAU, CÔTES DU RHÔNE-VILLAGES, FRANCE 321539 $17.60

FOUR AMAZING EVERYDAY RICH REDS

These wines are so good that they deserve awards.

Carmen's Cab is lighthearted and terribly gulpable. An interesting mix of gentle and rustic. Chilean Beaujolais! Will appeal most to those who enjoy a lighter touch in their rich reds. Drinkability and playfulness over heft. Perfect house wine.

If you're not already a Rhône fan, I think you will be after a few of sips of the Louis Bernard. So juicy, vibrant and charming – no worries. Should come with a `too easy to gulp´ warning.

Cono Sur has been rocking the wine world for a few years and the ten-dollar Shiraz is perhaps their most hedonistic wine yet. Lush, peppery, spicy and flying on freshness. Be prepared to be seduced. Sort of Rhône in style, just a bit more glitzy.

Hot off the boat is La Casona. A red with the peppery quality of Rhône and other good stuff too. The ultimate nine-dollar rich red! Certainly has the talent to challenge the current best sellers.

BEST TIMES: *Anytime!*

wine style: RICH RED UNDER $12

CARMEN 07 CABERNET SAUVIGNON, CHILE

78980 $10.75

wine style: RICH RED UNDER $12

LOUIS BERNARD 07 CÔTES DU RHÔNE, FRANCE

581645 $11.80

wine style: RICH RED UNDER $12

CONO SUR 08 SHIRAZ, CHILE 64295 $9.95

wine style: RICH RED UNDER $12

BODEGAS CASTANO 07 'LA CASONA', MONASTRELL, YECLA, SPAIN 143743 $8.95

Ri RICH RED

SHIRAZ IN THE FRENCH STYLE

Not all Shirazes are crafted in the yummy, fruity/spicy style. Some wineries favour a drier, more reserved style. Wine that's more at home on the dinner table than at the party. Wines with a French feeling.

`D'arry's Original´ has the refreshing, earthy, peppery quality of a Côtes du Rhône. Brisk and a little challenging at first, but a crusty, warmhearted character appears by the second glass. Will appeal to fans of traditional wines. Darenberg makes a lot of wines in the Rhône style, even some whites.

Cline labels their wine with the French spelling so you know what style to expect. Dry and refreshing, with a confident, elegant personality. Feels like a twenty-dollar wine.

BEST TIMES: *Exploring the Shiraz world.*

wine style: RICH RED

DARENBERG 06 SHIRAZ/GRENACHE 'D'ARRY'S ORIGINAL', MCLAREN VALE, AUSTRALIA

942904 VE $19.75

wine style: RICH RED

CLINE 07 SYRAH, SONOMA, CALIFORNIA

733758 VE $14.75

MATURE MEN

Most of today's red wines are best enjoyed in their fruity, youthful period. But a few can develop an appealing, mature character after a few years in bottle. I'm not a fan of very old reds with the flavours of overcooked meats, but I do love the early stages of maturity when fruity become earthy and a mellow sweetness develops.

Guigal is a traditional Rhône producer and his 05 Pinot combines the peppery qualities of the region with an exotic, seductive feeling. Very satisfying for late night sipping.

The Fontanafredda Barolo has a woodsy, fall-day-in-the-country feeling. Take a stroll and come home to a supper of roasted meat and veggies. An 'earth' day celebration. Barolo is somewhat similar to Pinot Noir in its pale colour and delicacy – more sensual than showy. No heft, but lots of charm.

BEST TIMES: *Late night supper or sipping.*

wine style: RICH RED

GUIGAL 05 CÔTES DU RHÔNE, FRANCE

259721 $17.80

wine style: RICH RED

FONTANAFREDDA 05 BAROLO, PIEDMONT, ITALY 20214 $29.85

RICHEST OF THE RICH

Every pleasure has its extreme performers – over-the-top stuff much loved by hedonists. Wines in this style are usually only found at specialty stores or at restaurants, but the LCBO does offer a few.

Mitolo is a relatively new Aussie winery that has a cult following for its blockbuster reds. The Shiraz has gorgeous berry pie flavours along with a lot of sweetness and richness. Too pretty for dinner but delicious for after – maybe with a chocolate truffle. Could be cellared for 3-5 years.

Mr. Blass' wine is also super-concentrated with Amarone-style richness. Lots of spicy sweet flavours, but very together. Another late night sipper, maybe with strong cheeses. Cellar potential here too.

Everyone seems to love Amarone and the current 06 vintage of Masi's wine is a showstopper. More winter warmth than a fireplace. Flavours seem to be a mile deep. Wine to nourish the body and soul. Will be even more exciting in 2-3 years.

BEST TIMES: *The full monty.*

wine style: RICH RED

MITOLO 07 SHIRAZ 'JESTER', MCLAREN VALE, AUSTRALIA 659607 VE $21.95

wine style: RICH RED

WOLF BLASS 06 SHIRAZ 'GREY LABEL', AUSTRALIA
390872 $34.95

Ri
RICH RED

wine style: RICH RED

MASI 06 AMARONE VALPOLICELLA 'COSTASERA', VENETO, ITALY 317057 $37.25

Sw

SWEET

EXOTIC
EXTRA STRONG
AFTERNOON
AFTER DINNER
OR BRUNCH
DELICIOUS
FINISH THE PARTY
SWEET
OR OFF DRY
SIPPERS
EXTRA EASY
NOVEL

SWEET WINES

OFF-DRY WHITES

Summer is the best season to enjoy this category of wines because of their garden-like flavours and lighthearted feeling, and because they are low in alcohol.

Between meals works because off-dry wines don't stimulate the palate, so we tend not to drink them as quickly as dry wines. Serve quite cold to balance the fruity sweetness.

Deinhard Riesling offers delicate flavours and gentle freshness – and a lazy afternoon feeling. Perfect for family gatherings or weekend brunches. Low alcohol.

Hardys wine also has a summer afternoon feeling. Light, airy and lazy. Refreshing notes mixed with delicious tropical fruit flavours. Could partner lunch too. Keep an open bottle in the fridge and I bet you'll find a hundred uses. Great value.

The 07 Jackson-Triggs Gewurz is richer and more flavourful than in the past. Some people suggest Asian food with this, but I get more of a late night sipping vibe – sunset with your sweetie.

BEST TIMES: *Off-dry wines offer a change of pace, which is what seasons are all about.*

wine style: OFF DRY

DEINHARD 07 RIESLING 'GREEN LABEL', MOSEL, GERMANY 8094 $11.15 UNDER $12

wine style: OFF DRY

HARDYS 08 RIESLING/GEWURZTRAMINER 'STAMP SERIES', AUSTRALIA 448548 $9.80 UNDER $12

wine style: OFF DRY

JACKSON-TRIGGS 07 GEWURZTRAMINER, VQA NIAGARA 526269 $11.95 UNDER $12

SEMI AND SWEET BUBBLY

It's easy to forget about sweet bubbly. Dessert wines and Port are always on the radar because they're a natural fit after dinner, but sweet bubbly is often forgotten. At least, by me.

But tasting for this book always reminds me of the pleasure to be had with fun bubblies such as Moscato, Fresita and Peller's amazing Ice Cuvée. Mark this page and return often.

Bottega Moscato is sweet, light and refreshing. Only 6% alcohol! Gorgeous Muscat flavours that make you think of summertime in the garden, or Christmas morning, or any good morning.

Fresita is a delicious, semi-sweet, strawberry-flavoured sparkling. Made with real fruit so there's no yukky artificial flavours – it's really quite refreshing. A must for brunch, or to celebrate whatever is rocking your world. Low alcohol too.

Peller Ice Cuvée Rosé sparkling is produced with a splash of Icewine. Could be the most delicious sparkler on the planet. It gets more wows than any other drink I pour. Perfect for before, during and after.

BEST TIMES: *Adding a little something to the moment.*

wine style: SWEET SPARKLING

BOTTEGA 'PETALO IL VINO DELL AMORE', MOSCATO, ITALY 588780 $12.95

wine style: SEMI-SWEET SPARKLING

VINA CASAL DE GORCHS 'FRESITA', CHILE
56697 $13.95

wine style: SEMI-SWEET SPARKLING

PELLER ESTATES ICE CUVÉE SPARKLING ROSÉ, VQA NIAGARA Vineyards Stores $32

Q: IN THE END, ISN'T IT ALL PERSONAL TASTE?

A: Yes and no. I've found if you pour the wine that's right for the mood, everyone will enjoy it. Personal taste will influence the degree to which people enjoy it but if it's right, it will work. Period. I've seen people go from hating to loving a wine when they experienced it in the right context. You might find this hard to believe, but it's true and happens often. Obsession with your likes and dislikes will keep you in your wine comfort zone, so you will be missing the potential magic of the moment. It's the connection between the wine and the moment that makes magic. Aim for this magic, welcome risk, chaos and the wilder side of wine.

Q: WHAT'S WITH SCREW CAPS, TETRA PAKS AND PLASTIC BOTTLES?

A: It's all good. Screw caps eliminate cork taint which causes wine to have a musty smell and taste (this happens to as much as 5% of all wines). They also prevent oxidation which dulls a wine. Wines with screw caps remain fresher and more flavourful – and you don't need a corkscrew. Cardboard and plastic containers are great for the outdoors or anywhere it's difficult to take a glass bottle. Too bad that most of these contain poor quality wine.

LITTLE BOTTLES OF SWEET

Icewine has become an Ontario speciality but we also produce really good sweet wines that are more reasonably priced. And more everyday. Wines with wonderful flavours and which manage to feel both refreshing and sweet.

I like to drink these wines cold because it tempers the sweetness. Serve in small, sherry-style glasses or whatever pleases you. Opened bottles will keep well for a week stored (hidden!) in the fridge.

For food ideas I suggest chocolate anything with the Framboise, and the other wines are delicious with biscotti, almond or lemon cake, or apple crisp. But on their own is also great.

Colio's Vidal has wonderful peach and caramel flavours and a refreshing tang. Best value sweet wine in the store – or world. Don't go to bed without a glass.

Cave's wine lives up to its name – late summer in a glass. Lively and lovely. Tons of rich, spicy fruit and a hit of refreshment. Another fun afternoon sipper. Will definitely take you somewhere.

If it's love in a glass you're after check out Pelham. Luscious with sweet, peachy flavours. This is a sweetie. The ideal little sip after a summer lunch in the garden, or late evening on the porch, or whenever you need to be reminded that life is sweet.

Framboise is liqueur-like wine made from raspberries. Wonderful with any chocolate dessert. Or just pour over ice cream – raspberries never tasted. Keep an open bottle in your fridge.

BEST TIMES: *Equally good in the winter or on a hot, sultry summer evening.*

UNDER $12 *wine style: SWEET*

COLIO ESTATES CEV 06 LATE HARVEST VIDAL, VQA ONTARIO 470369 $10.95 / 375ml

wine style: SWEET

CAVE SPRING 06 SELECT LATE HARVEST RIESLING 'INDIAN SUMMER', VQA ONTARIO 415901 $24.95 / 375ml

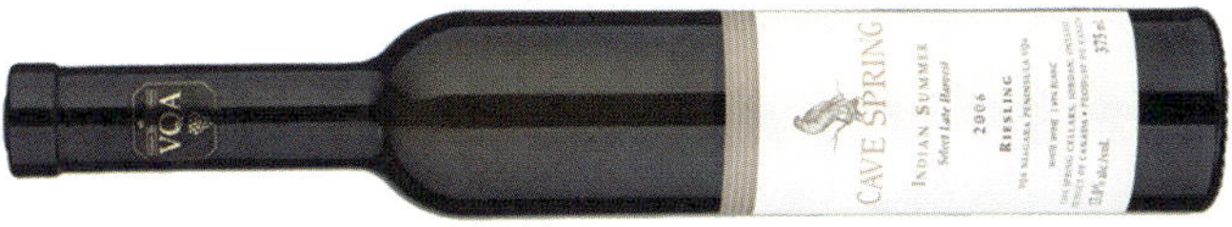

wine style: SWEET

HENRY OF PELHAM 06 LATE HARVEST VIDAL, VQA NIAGARA 395228 $19.95 / 375ml

wine style: SWEET

SOUTHBROOK WINERY FRAMBOISE, VQA ONTARIO

341024 $15.00 / 375ml

A GLASS OF PORT

PORT 101

Port continues to be one of the great values in wine when you consider the age, flavour concentration and overall character of what you're buying. Get some and celebrate something on a cold winter night.

The drink hails from the Douro River Valley in northern Portugal, where it gets hot as hell in summer so the grapes achieve huge ripeness. Port starts out as red wine but while it's still bubbling in the tank, brandy is added. This kills the fermentation and establishes the nature of Port – a red wine with some unfermented sugars and a fiery kick. A sweet and strong wine. Treat it with respect or you'll suffer the next day.

While there are many label designations for Port – too many – basically there are only two styles; dark, manly Ports known as Vintage-style, and pale, delicate, feminine, sensual Ports known as Tawny-style. Got that? Ports labeled Ruby are young, sweet editions of the Vintage style – fun, everyday stuff.

BEST TIMES: *Some enjoy Port with cheese, fruitcake or nuts, but I say best alone.*

BUYING WINE

YOUR LOCAL STORE

Don't be disappointed if you cannot find some of my recommendations at your local store. You can ask to have any wine ordered in.
Visit www.lcbo.com for product/store searches.

LCBO INFOLINE

For information on wine availability at any store call the LCBO Infoline. In Toronto, call 416.365.5900. Elsewhere you can call toll-free: 1.800.ONT.LCBO from 9 a.m. to 6 p.m., Monday to Saturday.

PRICE CHANGES

Because wine is produced in many different parts of the world, its price will tend to fluctuate more than that of shampoo. Prices given in this book are those at press time, but some may have changed by the time you shop. They do not include the 20¢ per bottle Ontario deposit.

LCBO VINTAGES

Vintages stores operate like a market in that new wines arrive on the shelves every two weeks, and when they're sold, they're gone. The ratio of good-to-boring wines is about the same at Vintages as at regular LCBOs – one in ten. Their beautiful catalogues try hard to make you believe otherwise. While one can get along quite nicely without Vintages wine, I recommend it to anyone with the enthusiasm for more variety. All the bigger LCBOs carry a selection of Vintages wines.

BUYING WINE ONLINE

Local wineries now offer shop-at-home service. If you'd like to buy a selection of wines from more than one winery, visit www.winerytohome.com. wineonline.com also offers local wines along with imports, including the wonderfully rustic Costieres de Nimes 06 `Barbabelle´ from France ($13).

BUYING FROM OTHER STORES

The Wine Rack, Vineyards Estates and Colio Wine Boutiques (located mainly in supermarkets) are worth visiting because they offer some interesting wines not available at LCBOs.

THE WINE RACK

Inniskillin, Jackson-Triggs, Le Clos Jordanne,
1.800.265.9463 www.winerack.com
Worth visiting for Jackson-Triggs `Delaine Vineyards´ and Clos Jordanne.

COLIO WINE BOUTIQUES

1.800.265.1322 or 519.738.2231
www.coliowinery.com
Colio's CEV line (from their own vineyards) offers some excellent premium wine at reasonable prices. Check out the tangy, herbaceous 06 Sauv Blanc ($16), and the charming, sipping 07 Gewurztraminer ($15) .

VINEYARDS ESTATE WINES

Hillebrand and Peller Estates
1.800.230.4321 www.vineyardestatewines.com
There are almost 100 Vineyards Estate wine stores throughout Ontario. Check out the value-priced Hillebrand `Artist Series´($12-$16). Peller's Ice Cuvée sparkling wines are made with a splash of Icewine – the Rosé ($32) may be the most delicious bubbly on the planet.

GRAPE CLASS 101

DRY RIESLING

Dry Riesling is the POW in cartoons. Low-flavoured but quick and to the point – it's the high notes, the tension during the final minutes of a closely contested sporting event. Have a glass to refresh. Have a second with sushi, and then move on to red wine. Re-cork and refrigerate the bottle. Repeat the next evening. Riesling originated in Germany. *(FYI Don't say rise-ling, say rees-ling)*

CHARDONNAY

Chardonnay is crafted in many style so it's a bit confusing. Non-oaked Chardonnay, much like Pinot Grigio, is great for light meals and everyday drinking. Chardonnay's ancestral home is the Burgundy region of France, but it was California and Australia that put Chardonnay on the map with their super-rich, exotic editions – Marilyn Monroe in a glass. The charred bitter flavours of BBQ'd foods and the spicy (sweet) flavours of rich Chardonnay play off really well with against each other. Or try a glass of blockbuster Chardonnay for a nightcap – often these wines are just too wonderful to share with food and conversation.

SAUVIGNON BLANC

Think Rock Star. Wine to get you going. Sauvignon is an energizing, edgy, sharp wine with an unusual herbal flavour. You might say it's a bit weird – something to love or hate. A first-of-the-day, and definitely the white wine that comes closest in style to a dry martini. If Chardonnay is carpet comfort, Sauv has the cold feeling of a marble-tiled floor. Most Sauvs now come in screw cap to guarantee freshness. New Zealand is the current big player, but look for Chile and South Africa to move up the charts. Niagara is doing well with this grape too.

PINOT GRIGIO

Simple-but-good wine for chillin' out. Pinot Grigio (PG) is the blue jeans of wine – everyday comfort and convenience. The easy solution. Could be likened to the early stages of a first date – wine to drink while you're feeling out the situation. Lightish wine for lighthearted times – daytime, early evening and family events. It really shines in the summer and although it doesn't need food, it can be a good partner for light meals or cream sauce dishes. Pinot Grigio hails from the northeast of Italy but (just to confuse you) also from Alsace, France. It's the light-hearted Italian model, however, that the rest of the world copies. There are many Grigio's recommended in this book. Keep an open bottle in the fridge.

GEWURZTRAMINER

Often described as the peacock, or drag queen of whites because of its showy, perfumed, exotic flavours. Alsace makes blockbuster Gewurz, while bottles from elsewhere are usually more restrained. Can be dry, medium or sweet. Fun in small doses or late at night.

P. S. Gewurztraminer is closely related to Muscat, the lord of exotic flavours.

GRÜNER VELTLINTER

Austria's national grape has become über-cool. Expect the zest of Sauvignon and the pure flavours of Dry Riesling. Wonderful hot day refresher or aperitif.

VIOGNIER

Another hot white grape variety. Pretty, charming and can be likened to Chardonnay with less makeup. Dry but can feel slightly sweet. Originated in the South of France.

VIDAL

A white hybrid developed to withstand the cold winters in northern France. Now the backbone of Ontario Icewine and other LateHarvest wines. Delicious tropical flavours and a hardy grower.

PINOT NOIR

Elusive. Expensive. Pinot Noir is a light red with a great capacity to stimulate the sensual side. More seductive than powerful. More fleeting than substantial. Lovers drink Pinot, warriors drink Cabernet. Pinot Noir originated in the Burgundy region of France where it still holds forth as one of the country's great reds. Unlike most red grapes, Pinot does not like heat so its travels have been mainly confined to cool regions such as New Zealand, Oregon and Ontario. Forget the beef – Pinot creates happy marriages with tons of other foods. Such as grilled salmon (a must try), mushroom risotto, Moroccan couscous, vegetarian fare, all the white meats, game and Tex/Mex dishes. It has a fondness for the exotic.

GAMAY

Lively and Lighthearted. Gamay's lively, fun nature and low alcohol makes it perfect for daytime drinking. Beaujolais is the prince of Gamay, the original and the only region in the world to grow the grape in large quantities. Ontario is one of the few other places to grow and make good Gamay. Hurray! The colour may be red but Gamay feels and acts a lot like white wine – it refreshes and delights. It's the child in the red wine family – full of energy and looking to play. We need Gamay in our lives so we don't forget to play – and to be reminded that we drink wine to become more lighthearted. Roast chicken and Gamay is very popular in France, but Gamay and cedar plank salmon on a summer evening is one of the all-time great wine pairings. Lightly chill Gamay to enhance its freshness – ten minutes in the freezer works.

SANGIOVESE

The Italian workhorse. Most of the red wines from the centre of Italy are produced from the Sangiovese grape, the most famous being Chianti from the province of Tuscany. In Tuscany, Sangiovese seldom gets mentioned on the label but you'll always see it on wines from the Abruzzi region. Mainly an everyday red to drink without fuss. Naturally, it's a great partner for the world of tomato sauced pasta and pizza. The premium editions should be paired with roasted or grilled meats. No sauces. The tartness in Sangiovese is also a good washdown for greasy foods such as burgers.

CABERNET SAUVIGNON & MERLOT

Lords of the reds. These guys originated in Bordeaux where it's the custom to make a blend of the two (plus a few other grape types). Cabernet is the most widely planted red grape variety in the world because of its reputation and because it travels well. In the old days, these were serious, very dry wines associated with British properness, men's clubs and roast beef. More recently, Cabernet Sauvignon and Merlot grapes were transplanted to the fun-loving New World – where they are crafted to be rich, smooth, slightly sweet and crowd-pleasing. Cabernet is supposedly the solid, manly type and Merlot the gentler, charming partner. However, it can be difficult to tell them apart

SHIRAZ/SYRAH

The darling red grape of this decade. Originated in France where it's called Syrah. Australia prefers Shiraz and other countries are confused or undecided. The Aussies developed Shiraz as a rich wine with lots of spicy/sweetness. A comforter and a crowd-pleaser that tastes and feels similar to the style of foods that most people enjoy – yummy, rich, sweet and instantly gratifying. Other regions (including Ontario) are producing a lighter, drier style, often labeled as Syrah. Have a glass or two of FRESH white or LIVELY red before getting into Shirazland. This is called wine foreplay. Even the Aussies do it. Also drink Shiraz after dinner, on the couch, by the fire – the high-alcohol feels nourishing and relaxing.

TEMPRANILLO

The grandad of Spanish reds such as Rioja and nearby Navarra and Priorato. Traditionally, it produced medium weight reds with tasty berry flavours but more recently it competes with all the other dark heavyweights.

ZINFANDEL

Originally from southern Italy (called Primitivo) this is America's fun, rich red. High-alcohol with tons of flavour but more roadhouse than steakhouse. And not in the least offended by sweet, spicy or hot sauces. Also crafted as a Blush wine just to confuse you.

MALBEC

Once part of the Bordeaux blend (along with Cabernet and Merlot) and now enjoying a rebirth as the signature red of Argentina. Tastes like Merlot on steroids, and not much different than all of today's rich reds.

GRENACHE

Seldom seen on the label, except in Australia. But this is the charmer behind Côtes du Rhône, lots of Spanish reds and the sexy Rosés from the South of France.

BACO NOIR

Ontario's rustic red. Wild, bitter and challenging. Great with a burger, but not for everyone. Check out Henry of Pelham from Niagara and Sandbanks from Prince Edward County.

WINE & FOOD SITUATIONS
A FEW HANDY RULES FOR ENTERTAINING

OFF TO A GOOD START
The first wine you serve at dinner, at a party, or even on a picnic, should be novel. A possible new experience for your guests. People are open to novelty at the beginning – they want a surprise. They know that you're going to give them something nice later. To provide novelty in the summer months, start with a chilled lively red. Give 'em Chardonnay later.

BEGIN WITH BUBBLY
With so many good, inexpensive sparkling wines around, it's a pity that more people don't start their events with a glass of something like Prosecco or Spanish Sparkling. Both are ideal partners for tapas or other Mediterranean appetizers. The acid and fizz in the wine make a refreshing swipe through the oil and garlic. They're also good with savoury pastry appetizers and with tempura or sushi.

THE BBQ
Serve wines that match the spirit of the food and event. Red meats need beefy reds. BBQ'd white meats welcome European reds such as Rhône, Beaujolais or anything Italian. Seafood and Chardonnay is a tradition, but for a change, try Semillon or Sauvignon Blanc.

WINE FOR CURRY
Try dry Rosé. I've found that it soothes the mouth without taking from the curry flavours. If anything, it expands the flavours – or allows your palate to experience them better. Shiraz seems to be popular at Indian restaurants, but it's not my favourite because it tries to outshine the food. For Thai green or red curry, check out Dry Riesling or a fresh Sauvignon Blanc.

...continued

HAPPY COUPLES

There are two possible action plans for pairing food with wine. The simplest is to pair wines and foods of similar personalities/moods – lighthearted with lighthearted, comfort with comfort, etc. The second approach is to work with contrasts, but this takes some skill and experience. Below are a few suggestions – all linked by MOOD, of course!

LIGHT 'N BRIGHT FOOD + LIGHT 'N BRIGHT WINE
a summer salad with VINHO VERDE

BRISK FOOD + BRISK WINE
pizza or colourful antipasto with BARBERA

BLAND FOOD + SPICY WINE
egg dishes with DRY MUSCAT or GEWÜRZTRAMINER

CHARRED FOOD + RICH/SWEET WINE
BBQ'd anything with RICH CHARDONNAY

CHARMING FOOD + CHARMING WINE
grilled salmon with BEAUJOLAIS or PINOT NOIR

GLAMOUR FOOD + GLAMOUR WINE
BBQ'd seafood with California Chardonnay

OILY FOOD + TART WINE
smoked salmon with ONTARIO DRY RIESLING

EXOTIC FOOD + EXOTIC WINE
Moroccan couscous with New World PINOT NOIR

SOFT FOOD + PERKY WINE
grilled burgers with ONTARIO GAMAY or BACO NOIR

MACHO FOOD + MACHO WINE
grilled steak with CABERNET SAUVGINON

COMFORT FOOD + SOULFUL WINE
roast chicken with CÔTES DU RHÔNE

TANGY FOOD + TANGY WINE
pasta in tomato sauce with young CHIANTI

SIMPLE FOOD + SAVOURY WINE
roasted or grilled chicken or pork with SEMILLON

BILLY'S 20 STEPS TO WINEDOM

ALL YOU NEED TO KNOW

1] HOW DOES IT FEEL

Wine and people are connected through feelings. Put aside the conventional belief that wine's statement is flavour – the essence or character of a wine can only be felt. It's the feeling of a wine that connects it to our moods and events.

2] EXERCISE DAILY

Make wine a daily companion. With so much wine to enjoy you'll never make a dent in it unless you drink it every day.

3] THINK ABOUT YOUR EXPERIENCE OF THE WINE, NOT THE WINE ITSELF

Different kinds of music create different emotional responses – this is also true of wine.

4] DO THE TWO-STEP

Most situations call for the wine two-step – refreshing wine to begin, and nourishing wine later.

5] MEET IT HALFWAY

Wine, like music, is interactive. Once you buy it (a bottle or a tune) the story is not complete until you experience it in the right context, mood and company. It's what YOU bring to the wine that will make it shine or not, and give it value. The ten-dollar bottle can deliver a hundred dollars worth of pleasure, and vice versa. Forget expertise and work on your playing skills. Aspire to become a good wine DJ.

6] ENJOY WINE FREELY

Get some experience and try lots of different wines at first. But avoid mental stress – you do not need to know wine to enjoy it. Knowing can come later.

7] EXPLORE BEYOND THE NICE & SMOOTH

Go beyond the top 40 hits. While easy wines provide comfort, the challenging ones keep us stimulated. Emotion and tension are as important in wine as in music. Entertain lots of wine moods, such as:

CHALLENGING: DRY RIESLING
LIVELY: VALPOLICELLA
MELLOW: AMARONE
SOULFUL: CHIANTI
WILD: SAUVIGNON BLANC
CHARMING: PINOT NOIR
GLAMOROUS: OAKED CHARDONNAY
PLAYFUL: BEAUJOLAIS/GAMAY,
SEXY: MERLOT
ADVENTUROUS: ANYTHING NEW

8] AVOID PRESTIGE WINE

And the mob that follow it. Wine attracts a lot of snobs, geeks and people with too much money. The mind of the snob drinker tells him to like the snob wine. The mind of the novice is free to support the good feeling of an everyday wine.

9] MAKE A MATCH

Good times do not need great wine – just the one that works for the mood and moment. Matching wine and moment is what creates good times, not the price of the bottle.

10] LEARN BY CONTRAST

Have several wines on the go so you can experience contrasting styles. And discover how there is always one wine that's better for the moment than the rest. Open, refrigerated wines keep well for 3 to 5 days.

11] GET OFF TO A GOOD START

The first wine that you serve at a dinner or party should be novel – a possible new experience for your guests. People are open to novelty at the beginning – they want a surprise. They know that you are going to give them something nice later.

12] BE PLAYFUL

Drinking should be one of our most playful times, so let playful wines be your main purchase.

13] MATCH WINE WITH FOOD & MOOD

If you are drinking the wine that's right for your mood, it will also be right for the food. Because you will have made a food choice based on your mood. Got that?

14] KEEP YOUR TALK PLAIN

Many people have difficulty expressing their feelings about a wine because they believe there is a correct response to each wine. They fear giving the wrong answer. If a wine feels happy, comforting, or dreary, go ahead and say so. These are more meaningful expressions than what the experts come up with.

15] THE TWO WINE CAMPS

Wine can be divided into two camps – the Old World wines and the New World wines. Old World wines (France, Italy, etc.) are typically very dry and are often challenging. But, like European movies they can be thought-provoking. New World wines (California, Australia, etc.) are easier to like and they taste a lot sweeter. These are crafted to appeal to a culture that drinks a lot of fruit juice and pop. New World wines work well with a lot of today's spicy/hot foods while Old World wines are happiest with traditional roasts and grills.

16] IN CASE OF EMERGENCY...

Grab the Beaujolais. Get a baguette (and maybe some Brie). Leave your worries on the doorstep. Take your picnic to the sunny side of the street.

16] BE OPEN-MINDED & TAKE CHANCES

Seek out new experiences, something you've not had before. Wine is about change – it helps us change. It's a great outlet for imagination. And of course for relaxation, contemplation, communion and enchantment.

18] CELEBRATE THE EVERYDAY – IN WINE & LIFE

Wine's origins are in peasant culture – an old wooden table, the shade of a tree and good company. Wine is about sociability and celebrating the everyday.

19] THERE ARE NO BEST WINES

Only wines that are best for the moment.

20] IT'S THE TRIP THAT COUNTS

Chart your own course. Enjoy the good times and keep learning from what didn't work. It will always be a bit confusing, a bit challenging – just like life. Which is part of the excitement. Enjoy.

WINE INDEX

OVER 200 WINES BY COUNTRY

ONTARIO

BRITISH COLUMBIA

ARGENTINA

AUSTRALIA

AUSTRIA

CHILE

FRANCE

GERMANY

HUNGARY

ITALY

billy's best bottles
'BOWLING FOR BEAUJOLAIS'
bocce champions